COLLATERAL DAMAGE

MAFIA ELITE, BOOK 6

AMY MCKINLEY

ARROWSCOPE PRESS, LLC

(p) ISBN-13: 978-1-951919-29-0

(e) ISBN-13: 978-1-951919-28-3

Publisher: Arrowscope Press, LLC; www.arrowscopepress.com

Editing— Kate Birdsall, Line Editor, Taylor Anhalt, Proofreader, Red Adept Editing

Cover Design—T.E. Black Designs; www.teblackdesigns.com

Author photo provided by—Brookelyn Anhalt of lovely.life.photography; https://www.facebook.com/LovelyLifePhotography-102253596490708

Interior Formatting & Design— Arrowscope Press, LLC; www.arrowscope-press.com

THE FAMILY

**Chicago Outfit
Italian American Mafia**

Caruso Family
Maximus "Max" (boss, married Liliana Brambilla)
Elena (sister, married Marco La Rosa)
Tony (Max's half-brother)
Parents/former boss
Antonio – (father, former boss, deceased)
Maria (first wife to Antonio, deceased, Max's Mom)
Nicole (second wife to Antonio, Tony's Mom, Elena's adopted Mom)
Vito (advisor to boss)
Maria's family from Italy
Salvio "Sal" (cousin)
Cristiano (cousin)
Tommasso (cousin)
Aunt Rosa (lives in Sicily)

Brambilla Family
Luca "Luc" (boss, married Summer)
Liliana "Lil" (half-sister, married Max Caruso)
Sal (underboss, cousin)
Dino (advisor to boss)
Eva (cousin, deceased)
Parents/former boss
Benito (former boss, deceased)
Julia (Benito's wife, deceased)
Vincenzo (Julia's Sicilian father, Liliana's grandfather)

La Rosa Family
Marco (boss, married Elena Caruso)
Nico (underboss, brother)
Trey (brother)
Sofia (sister, married Enzo Vitale)
Maso (Robert's brother, advisor)
Tom (captain)
Parents/former boss
Robert (former boss)
Angela (Robert's wife)

Vitale Family
Enzo (boss, married Sofia La Rosa)
Emiliana "Em" (sister, married Stefano Rossi)
Aldo (advisor to boss)
Renato "Ren" (captain)
Parents/former boss

Emilio (former boss)
Alessia (Emilio's wife)

Rossi Family
Stefano (boss, married Emiliana Vitale)
Camila (sister, married Vic Pavlov)
Alfonso (brother, deceased)
Marissa (sister, deceased)
Drago (advisor to the boss)
Parents/former boss
Frank (father, former boss, deceased)
Carla (Frank's wife, deceased)

Russian Mafia
Pavlov Bratva

Pavlov Bratva
Yuri (boss)
Mischa (wife)
Ivan (eldest son, former underboss, deceased)
Victor "Vic" (son, underboss, married Camila Rossi)
Katya (angel of death, assassin)

New York Outfit
Italian American Mafia

Amato Family
Leo (boss)
Guido (son, underboss)
Ben (cousin, soldier, deceased)

Tucci Family
Joey (boss)
Linda (2nd wife)
Ricco (step-son, underboss, Linda's son)
Mia (daughter)

Verretti Family
Dante (boss)
Calvino "Cal" (brother, underboss)
Adriano (youngest brother, assassin)

CHAPTER ONE

HAILEY

I'd prepared for the last two weeks, and I was ready for the big moment. I flattened a hand on my stomach in an attempt to settle my nerves. I sat in my parked car, close to the hospital's entrance, where I would meet my stepfather, nervous because I had to leave just the right impression.

I'd taken care with my outfit and not worn my typical jeans with holes at the knees and an oversized sweatshirt. Not this time. My curly hair was tamed as best as possible with a clip at my nape to secure the long mass. I'd even added mascara and a soft-pink lipstick to my arsenal of business attire—pencil skirt, blouse, and matching blazer—that was very unlike me.

The heat blasted through the car's vents, and I wished I'd worn boots instead of the ridiculous heels, as it was icy out. January weather in Chicago was hell-frozen-over cold. I missed summer.

Movement near the entrance caught my eye, and I tensed and reached for the door handle as Mom's second husband closed in on the building.

This is it. Allen Mitchel, you have no idea what you're in for.

I opened the door, rounded the car, and kept my stepfather

in sight as I hurried through the parking lot and across the street, toward the doors he was about to enter. My heels crunched over salt and pockets of ice that hadn't yet melted. A shiver raced over me, and my breath formed a small misty cloud.

"Allen." I still couldn't call him Dad. He hadn't even slowed, and I gritted my teeth before saying his name again, much louder this time. "Allen!"

He turned. *Finally.* Then his eyes widened, fixated on something past my shoulder, and my step faltered.

Tires screeched, and I froze. My heart skipped a beat—the car skidding behind me could have hit me. Then a door slammed. I took a step forward, looking over my shoulder only to glimpse a black ski mask.

Rough hands grabbed me and jerked my body back against a lean chest as I opened my mouth to scream.

CHAPTER TWO

TREY

Exhaustion shadowed my every step into the ER. The omnipresent scent of antiseptic enveloped me, and I inhaled its familiarity while heading to the nurses' station for any new information about my patients.

Britney, one of the nurses, waved from down the corridor, quickening her pace the closer she got to me. "Dr. La Rosa." Her mouth formed a small O as she tripped on nothing, but her eyes telegraphed excitement. I caught her by the arms, making sure she was steady and not about to fall into me before I removed my hands.

"Thank y—"

"Britney." Sandy's sharp tone preceded her as she drew alongside us, having just entered the ER floor. Her shift must have started at the same time as mine. "Go check on your patients."

Brittney hesitated, her big doe eyes lingering before she reluctantly turned away when I didn't contradict the head nurse's orders.

"Honestly"—exasperation colored Sandy's voice—"these young nurses have no shame."

"It's not that bad."

"Not that bad?" Her head whipped around until her sharp eyes landed on me. "When you're not watching, they look at you like you're a piece of meat. I can't even tell you how many times I've had to rearrange the schedule to make sure the worst of your fans aren't on shift when you are. They need to stop planning their weddings with you and focus on their jobs."

I offered a sheepish smile, itching to get started on rounds. Sandy was worth her weight in gold, but it wasn't a conversation I liked having.

"You're the trifecta of all catches, a dangling carrot to the younger ones." She grunted as Peggy called a breathy good morning before going into one of the rooms. "And a few of the not so young ones too."

I shouldn't have asked but couldn't help myself: "Trifecta?"

She ticked off her fingers as she listed them. "Gorgeous. A prestigious surgeon. And of course, the Mafia. All that with the added bonus of a surgeon's salary and the substantial Mafia-funded bank account with a dash of white knight and a side of bad boy, and these women are toast."

I chuckled. "Good thing I've got you on my side." I meant it. She was the most efficient charge nurse in the hospital and kept her staff in line. I didn't need to have a discussion with any of the nurses in question, whose seemingly innocent touches lingered a little too long.

She winked, clearly enjoying my discomfort, then stepped away as the phone on the main desk rang but flung her arm out toward one of the patient rooms. I followed her, needing to check the notes regarding any of the patients who hadn't been discharged yet from the doctor who'd worked the shift before me.

Sandy was the only nurse I let in and cared enough for to ask how she was doing. I went about my job with efficiency and a demeanor that didn't invite conversation from the hospital staff unless it was about work. Lately, I'd been like that in most areas of my life.

It hadn't always been that way. I joked with my family and did everything I could to keep them from seeing how my heart had just about stopped beating after Teresa, the barista I'd dated from the Coffee Stop, died. Sofia, my sister, was the only one who knew how deeply her death slayed me or that I still hadn't recovered from it. Our relationship had been a secret. Mostly. I'd wanted to keep her from my world, and all she'd wanted was me. She was pure. Happy. Innocent. A complete anomaly in my world.

No one is innocent.

I couldn't get enough of her until somebody took her from me, and I hadn't been the same since.

Outwardly, everyone but Sofia thought I was fine, and she'd given me the space I'd told her I badly needed. I threw myself into my work. It was what saved me.

Jaded but still passionate about what I did outside of my Mafia responsibilities, I geared up to focus on the patients I would be helping. I had a light shift, and after the chaos with the ambush organized by Guido Amato, one of the New York Mafia underbosses, I needed to regroup and log a few more hours of sleep—preferably without the world imploding with my family or at the hospital where I was staffed.

Something was different, and a sixth sense sounded an internal alarm that snapped me from my thoughts. My instincts flared. A surge of adrenaline shot through me, erasing the indifference and fatigue. My gaze darted around the busy floor as I cataloged everything out of place—it was in the silence as the staff went about their jobs and the absence of triage. No codes were called. The air was heavy, a sense of somberness significant in the lack of smiles or gossip at the nurses' station and the pallor of Sandy's face as she hung up the phone.

The pen in her hand shook before she set it down. Her big

blue eyes were devoid of all teasing when they met mine, which was highly unusual. I slid a hand inside my open lab coat and around the back, where I'd tucked my gun in the waistband of my pants. "Sandy." I approached her slowly, noting the tremble in her lower lip. "What's the problem this morning?"

"Mr. Mitchel asked that you see him immediately." Her voice cracked.

Allen Mitchel ran the hospital. He didn't deserve the position, but his marriage to Vanessa Carmichael had afforded him the honor, as her family owned the hospital among other businesses, including Chicago's prized professional hockey team.

I took the elevator up to the top floor, where the executive staff offices were. Once off the elevator, I headed down the hall toward Allen's door. Two Chicago police officers exited his office, and I nodded to them. Their eyes were wary with recognition, but they returned the greeting.

Allen's door was open. Not bothering to knock, I let myself in then towered over his slumped form at his desk. I waited, not saying a word. Being summoned by him wasn't something I would typically respond to, but Sandy's reaction had propelled me to see what the issue was. Seeing cops leave made me curious.

Slowly, he raised his head. I took in the disheveled hair that on an average day was smoothed to perfection, the red-rimmed eyes, and the loosened tie. I stood silently, waiting.

"Trey." He cleared his throat then swiped a hand through his hair, mussing it further. "I know we've had our differences."

I grinned—couldn't help it. He threw a lot of shade in my direction without outright calling me out. I knew his arrogant type. He thought he was better than everyone else because of his position and he'd married into money. I wasn't impressed.

"Yes, well." A spark of annoyance flashed across his drawn features, tightening them at my response. "Today, I was to meet my daughter to talk about having her spearhead the hospital fundraiser this spring." He inhaled through his nose, taking a moment to compose his suddenly misty eyes. "She never made it."

The news hit me hard, but I kept my face expressionless. "That's why the police were here?"

He nodded, his forehead pinched with deep lines. "I'll have to go to the station soon to give a statement, but I fear she won't be found in time."

Is she dead? That was what it seemed he had been leading up to. "I have things to do, Allen. Stop playing games and tell me what you're talking about without the melodrama."

A dark flash filled his eyes then disappeared so quickly that most would have discounted it. I filed that away for later. Whatever was going on, he was hiding something.

"I was almost inside the hospital entrance when Hailey crossed from the parking lot. She'd called out to me, and I turned just as a white van pulled up behind her. A man dressed in black and wearing a ski mask jumped out and grabbed her. He threw her into the back and drove away before I could get to her."

The Carmichael family were one-percenters. I guessed that the abduction was about money. "What does this have to do with me?" It didn't. I was curious why he'd told me anything, especially since he'd made it so evident that I shouldn't be on staff at the hospital—his snobby disposition had telegraphed his opinion loud and clear. I'd let it go, not caring enough to put him in his place. Despite his executive position, he was a peon, and he didn't do any actual work. No one took him seriously.

"I want you to find her."

"I don't think so." I smirked at the ridiculousness of his request, even though I knew damn well I would find her—but without his help. "Let the cops do their job." I pivoted to leave.

"Wait."

I stopped, rested my shoulder against the doorjamb, and

watched as he froze in a half-standing position behind his desk, desperation pulling his hawklike aristocratic features taut.

"Her abductor called me with a ransom demand. They want ten million for Hailey's safe return. We have seventy-two hours. No police."

That was a longer time than I would have expected. "She's already dead, then, as you've involved the cops."

"They were only here because one of the security guards witnessed Hailey's abduction. I haven't shown the police the security tape. I told them there was a glitch and nothing recorded."

A sheen of sweat gathered along his upper lip, and the killer instinct in me honed to laser focus. "Who else knows about your little misdemeanor, Allen?"

"No one. I swear."

"And Hailey's mother? Have you told her what happened on your watch?"

The same darkness from before clouded his eyes for a second then was gone again. Allen gave a single shake of his head.

It piqued my curiosity enough that I entertained looking at the security footage. "Show me."

He slid his computer over then pressed the play button. The recording was of the area in front of the hospital's entrance. The camera angle captured the space beneath the overhang and toward the parking lot.

A young woman hurried through the lot. Something unexpected stirred in my heart at the sight of her—the memory of when we'd first met. I resisted rubbing at the odd sensation in my chest. I couldn't look away from the recording as she called to Allen, who had paused beneath the entrance's overhang when she spoke to him a second time.

He turned, his back to the camera as a white van barreled down the road then screeched to a stop, inches from where she stood. A tall, lean man with broad shoulders hopped out. Dressed all in black and with a ski mask covering his face, he ran to the woman, whose back was still to him. As she looked over her shoulder, he jerked her body back into his, and I tensed in response. Both his arms wound around her tiny waist. She kicked out, scrambling for purchase to get away. A stiletto fell off her foot, and she opened her mouth to scream. He tightened his hold around her and her lungs. From her expression, the air was limited, and sound must have failed her.

As they moved toward the back of the van, he lifted her inches from the ground, and she kicked wildly despite being secured against his chest. One arm loosened, and he wrenched open the van's back door.

Allen shifted slightly. One step forward, a hand outstretched.

The man flung a hood over the woman's head before tossing her into the back. Doors slammed just as a security guard barreled from the hospital's entrance. He was too late. Hailey's attacker took his seat behind the wheel. *Odd.* The tires spun before they found purchase, and the vehicle lurched forward. Soon, it was out of sight. Allen had barely moved from his spot under the overhang.

I paused the video then rewound it to when her attacker lifted her then tossed her in the back. She'd stopped fighting— only for a second, but it was enough to stand out. I let it play out then went back to the scene again.

When the recording ended, I couldn't hold back the memory of how I'd first met Hailey. I'd been at a party with Marco and Sofia, who had gone to get a refill on drinks. Nico hadn't been able to attend. While I appreciated that my family had accompanied me to the hospital's leukemia fundraiser, all I wanted to do was go home, sleep, and forget why my heart hurt. I leaned against the wall as the clink of heels vied with conversation, and an edgy awareness danced over my skin.

Every muscle in my body tightened in reaction, and I

scanned the dance floor for its cause. Everything paused as I spotted a stunning woman in a black satin evening gown. A high slit in her dress revealed a toned golden leg, and diamonds dripped from her ears.

I recognized her. How could I not have? Her mother, Vanessa Carmichael, owned the hospital.

My vision tunneled as the temptress in black satin and diamonds headed my way. All the depressing thoughts that had taken residence in my mind, urging me to leave, fled as she crossed the edge of the dance floor in strappy three-inch silver heels When she was about a foot from me, our gazes collided, and she faltered as an electrical current passed between us.

I angled my body toward her and extended my hand. "I don't believe we've been officially introduced. I'm Trey La Rosa."

She placed hers in mine, and a jolt of desire buzzed through me.

"Hailey Carmichael. And I know your sister."

"My sister's been holding out on me." Her full red lips curved into a smile, and I stepped closer. "Would you like to dance?"

She answered with a light nod, and I pulled her close and stepped onto the dance floor to a haunting and evocative violin concerto. Her skin was soft beneath my hands as we swayed together, her slender body enticing me to press her tight to mine.

But we were at a party where there were too many sets of eyes on us. Long lashes lifted, and I found myself drowning in a sea of shimmering gemstone green. "I haven't seen you at the hospital fundraisers before tonight. Why is that?"

A flash of something flitted across her face—maybe annoyance. It piqued my interest and made me wonder whether she was there with someone or if the irritation had to do with her family.

"I was away at school. But I'm sure I'll be attending more if my mother has anything to do with it." Her voice dropped to a whisper, and intelligence spiked with mischief sparkled through her expressive eyes. "Truth be told, this isn't my scene."

I grinned, enjoying myself for the first time that evening. "The pompous gathering of socialites or raising money for a cause?"

She chuckled, shaking her head. Her thick, wavy hair bounced from side to side. "The cause is not the issue. But I would much rather simply write a check."

"Hm." I couldn't blame her. The night was long, and we still had to get through the speeches.

One song turned into five as we talked and danced, cocooned in one another's arms. When the song ended and the band announced that they were taking a break, I led her off the dance floor to where my sister was waiting for us.

"Hailey." Sofia drew her into a hug.

"How is it that you never introduced us?" My hand never left the small of Hailey's back, the contact somehow grounding me, chasing away the emotions that had plagued me before.

Sofia shrugged then took a sip of her champagne. "I meant to. I'm surprised you haven't run into us having coffee."

An unwanted jolt of pain pierced through the bubble that Hailey had managed to gift me with that one word. "Where?"

Sofia flinched. Hailey answered instead. "At the Coffee Stop."

Teresa. The spell Hailey had cast over me shattered, and reality crashed into my world once more. That was where Teresa had worked. Then she'd dated me. Then she died. My hand fell away, and I took a step back, crushing guilt defining my actions. *How could I have forgotten, if even only for a few moments?*

I turned on my heel and walked away, my former girlfriend's ghost haunting my every step, along with the phantom sound of Teresa's infectious laughter. In my peripheral vision, I saw Sofia wrap an arm around Hailey, whose face had registered acute rejection as they made a hasty retreat out of the gala.

It was for the best.

I clenched my jaw and jerked free of the memory, refocusing on the screen in front of me and the overwhelming need to help Hailey.

The abduction had happened in a matter of seconds, but I knew seeing her again had altered my life somehow.

I didn't like it. I hadn't been ready for her then, and I doubted I was now.

Allen's hand shook as he pressed another button, switching to a different camera angle, and I watched the entire thing all over again. I paused the video. I went back to the first one with a few clicks, found a frame that worked for what I wanted, then enlarged a section to see her face. My gaze crawled over her stunning face, slender figure, and dark hair.

"You look nothing alike." I'd done my homework on him a long time ago and knew enough. Both mother and daughter had kept their surname, and Allen had attempted to manipulate my emotions by saying his *daughter* was missing—Allen and Hailey weren't related by blood. I couldn't help needling him. I doubted he had much if anything to do with how she was raised. His arrogant I've-got-a-silver-spoon-stuck-up-my-ass demeanor had nothing on the captivating woman with features I knew would haunt my dreams again tonight.

"I hardly see how it matters whether we look alike or not." Allen bristled, clearly unaware that I'd met Hailey in the past. "She's my stepdaughter. But that hardly matters. We are family."

While I was curious about the woman, I had no desire to do anything for her stepfather unless I got something in return.

He pursed his lips, his body equally tense. "Will you help find her?"

"No. Leave it to the police." I turned to go.

"What? They said not to." Allen ran a shaky hand over his face. "You have to find her before the time limit runs out. They said…" He trailed off, his face going sickly gray.

Silence hung between us as I paused by the door. Desperation oozed from him. Again, I turned to leave.

"Wait." He sneered. "I'll give you a seat on the board."

If I wanted that, I would already have it. I shook my head. I was going to help her, preferably without his knowledge. I glanced at the computer. Then again, he could believe I wanted a seat on the board if it kept my motivations hidden. "Make a copy of the security footage now. I want to take it with me."

"You'll help?" He slumped back, relief slackening his features.

Yes. I said nothing as he fumbled to insert a USB drive and copy the two videos.

He shook his head. "I just want the safe return of my step-daughter. But nothing can trace back to me. If you kill the kidnappers, it will. This needs to be clean—no deaths."

I raised my eyebrows, and Allen's face flushed.

"You took an oath."

I laughed. He knew who I was and where my loyalties lay.

Allen leaned forward, clutching the edge of his desk. "Promise me, no deaths."

I closed the distance between us, flattened my hands on the mahogany surface, and loomed over him. "Be careful how you talk to me, Allen. You won't like the repercussions." I held his gaze long enough to convey what I would do to him should he press me further. "Make it happen with the board, and I'll see what I can do about your daughter."

A glance at the screen showed the recording was copied. I ejected the drive and pocketed it, patting Allen's cheek before I left his office. I meant what I said. I would look into the situation. He wasn't counting on my finding out what he wasn't telling me, though. There was something very off about the footage of Hailey's abduction.

CHAPTER THREE

TREY

After leaving Allen's office, I forwarded the footage from Hailey's abduction to Nico then went about seeing patients. He would require time to search through the traffic camera feeds and any others he needed to hack. Hailey remained in my thoughts, but I had someone special to check in on, and I had to concentrate on her rather than a disturbing video of a woman who piqued my interest.

"Mrs. Armond." I stood by the bedside of a seventy-year-old who had stolen my heart years ago from the moment she'd waltzed into the ER and demanded to be seen. I'd recognized her instantly as a good friend and makeup artist of my mother's who worked in the industry while Mom did a few shows in the States. Mom would be in later to visit, and I looked forward to seeing her. "How are you feeling?" I logged in to Mrs. Armond's electronic chart and scanned the test results that Sandy told me had just arrived.

"*Katherine*. Stop making me feel old," she admonished then sighed dramatically with a mischievous glint sparkling in her faded blue eyes. "Room service was atrocious, and don't get me started on the sheets."

I chuckled. "I'll see what I can do about that." I leaned close and added in a conspiratorial whisper, "Don't tell the other patients. You know they'll be jealous."

"Of extra attention from Dr. Hottie?"

My eyebrows rose before I barked out a laugh. "Don't repeat ridiculousness."

She sniffed. "The nurses like to gossip. It's impossible not to hear them."

"I have eyes only for you. Ignore them." I flirted shamelessly with her, avoiding giving her the news for as long as I could. The amusement fell from her aging face. She was on to me.

"Give it to me straight, Doc. I've lived a long life, and I know when something is very wrong. It's back, isn't it?"

Leukemia. I closed my eyes for a moment, gathering strength to give bad news to an old woman my family hadn't seen in too many years. Soon, her boisterous family would infiltrate our hospital in droves to surround her with laughter. "Yes."

Tears misted her eyes, but she blinked them away. Stubbornness that would rival my sister's took its place. "How long?"

"I don't want to define your life in what you have left when there's another option." I'd scoured the doner lists and then placed a few calls last night, and if she agreed, I had a solution for her. It could save her if she was willing. If her family was. "When are your son and daughter going to be here?"

"We aren't doing that, young man." Katherine struggled to sit up, and I helped her, arranging the pillows so she was comfortable. "I'm of sound mind. Lay it on me."

"I found a match. But"—I held up a finger to stop her from making a hasty decision—"the bone marrow donor is in Europe. Italy, to be specific. And I have connections there. You'll have to undergo a few more tests once you're there."

She patted my hand. "I know all about your connections, Trey. But I fail to see how that will help. Isn't there a match in the States?"

I shook my head. There wasn't. "Mom will insist that you go when I tell her, and you know she can be a force, just like you. Don't think she won't have you kidnapped and transported to Italy during the night."

"She was always my favorite of all the models." Katherine's sigh held a longing I felt deep in my bones for what was. "How is that firecracker of a sister of yours?"

I laughed. "Sofia is a handful, but she's married and no longer causing our brothers or me hell."

"Such a darling girl." She patted my cheek then glanced at my ringless hand. "And you? Are you engaged yet?"

"No one's managed to catch my eye." I sat on the side of her bed, knowing my statement to be a bald-faced lie. "Stop changing the subject. This is what we're going to do. Mom will be here this afternoon to help you and your kids pack what you want to bring on your trip to Italy. If you want one of your family members to go with, that's fine, but you'll be in good hands there and staying with Vincenzo Brambilla, a friend of our family's."

Interest lit her eyes. "Why would another Mafia family want to help a stranger?"

"His granddaughter Liliana is my sister's close friend, and we all have history. He's one of the good ones. I promise he'll take care of you."

"If I agree to this, what are the chances of remission?"

Of a cure. "Very good. There's a high chance of success."

"And the hospital there? Insurance? How will that work?"

It wouldn't. And I knew she didn't have the funds to cover even a small portion of it. "You're a friend of the family. It'll be handled. You'll have a private nurse and a sterile room that isn't in a hospital. There is nothing for you to worry about." Her chin quivered, and I didn't want to cause her any distress, so I gently squeezed her hand. "Mom will be here to help smooth things over with your family. The jet leaves before dinner, and my parents will be with you on the flight over and to make sure you're settled in Vincenzo's estate." Traveling to a stranger's home and out of the country was enough to rattle anyone's nerves. Stress was the last thing Katherine needed. I had a feeling she'd quite like Vincenzo, though. "Mom will stay as long as you want her to." I chuckled. "Good luck getting rid of her. I'm pretty sure my parents are looking for a house in Italy, so you're doing them a favor."

She nodded once. It was enough for me to finalize the plans I had in motion. "It's settled, then." I knew how hard it was for her to accept anything she thought was a handout, but this was her life, and I was glad she'd agreed.

She sagged against the pillows, and I smiled reassuringly. "Your discharge papers will be in order soon, but you'll have until about four this afternoon before it's time to leave." That gave her enough time to figure out what she wanted to have packed and brought to stay in Italy.

"Trey"—her using my first name caused a flood of memories to surface. There were so many of my siblings and me playing at her and Mom's feet while Katherine did Mom's hair and makeup for a fashion shoot she'd agreed to attend—"why are you doing this?"

"Doing what?"

"Working in a hospital? Don't forget, I may have been absent for the last few years and living in another state, but I know your family."

She'd always been a smart cookie. I winked, wanting to add some levity to our discussion. "Putting in my dues. I won't be here much longer, but it was good that I was when you came in yesterday." If I hadn't been, none of us would have known about Katherine's stay, and my mother would have been devastated if we hadn't helped her.

One of the nurses walked in, and I gave her instructions about monitoring Katherine's IV and giving her a pain reliever.

She would need to be hydrated and comfortable for the long flight tonight. Dinner would be on the jet, and I knew she would be happier with the food they would serve over the hospital's. I left detailed notes with Sandy, who I ensured would be there to handle everything before her shift ended.

After Katherine's papers were in order, I took the next few hours to finish my rounds. An eleven-year-old boy had needed stiches on his forehead after a skateboarding fall at one of the indoor parks. A woman was brought in after a car accident but had gotten off lucky with only bruises and a broken arm. I'd set the arm and given her a prescription for painkillers to cover a few days. After that, the floor was quiet, and as soon as my shift was over, I headed out of the hospital. Worry for what Hailey was going through returned full force once I wasn't preoccupied with patients.

It was time to meet with Nico.

***

Once inside my Maserati, I connected my Bluetooth and hit the button to dial my brother Nico. He answered on the third ring.

"I found her." Nico's deep voice clipped through the speakers. "Not her exact location but the neighborhood. I'll get that narrowed down by the time you get here. And I haven't had a chance to do a thorough background check on her yet."

The video nagged at me again. "What did you notice right before he tossed her into the back of the van?"

"I saw the hesitation, too, but we can't see his mouth from either angle in the recordings. It's possible her kidnapper said something to make her freeze. Or they know each other."

"Yeah, that's what's been bothering me. Find out if anyone in the area you've identified has a connection to her or Allen."

I disconnected and let Nico do his thing. The guy could hack into the Pentagon if he wanted. I had no doubt he would have the information I'd asked for and then some in a matter of minutes.

I needed to strategize with my brothers. In the back of my mind, the distrust I felt for Allen festered, and I shot off a text telling Nico I would be there soon.

About forty minutes later, I pulled into the long driveway that led to my parents' house. Marco had his place with Elena, but Nico and I stayed with them for the most part, at least for the time being. That would change, but he wasn't in a hurry to leave—the house was a mansion, and our parents traveled a lot. I couldn't blame him, as I did the same thing. I owned a greystone in the city and crashed there when I needed to, but staying at the family home was easier, especially with hospital hours, and we were Italian—family was everything.

The subdivision was gated, and after bypassing the guardhouse, I weaved through the streets until I came to our sprawling home. Security patrolled the grounds. Rather than pull into the garage, I parked in front, got out, and nodded to the guards posted by the door. Once inside, I didn't waste any time and went straight to where I knew Nico would be—his office in the east wing. He had a computer setup to rival the National Security Agency's.

I entered without knocking. Three large monitors took up one portion of the desk, and he'd situated himself behind them, typing at a pace I couldn't match even if I'd wanted to.

"What took you so long?" Nico peered around the side of the closest monitor.

I snorted then fell into a chair opposite him.

"I found the house," Nico said, and my focus sharpened as I waited to hear more. "Blinds are all closed, and I counted two cameras that cover both doors, front and back." After rattling off the address so that I would have it, Nico turned one of the screens around so that I could see. A frown marred his face.

"The house is registered to Justin Redford. He's on the list I'd compiled of Hailey's friends and family. He's a friend."

"Boyfriend?" The question came out before I could stop it, and a grin I didn't like curved my brother's lips.

"Why? Are you interested in her?"

I grabbed a pen off his desk and tossed it at his head, but he caught it before it could make impact. "Just tell me."

"No. Justin's romantic interests are in line with what Hailey's probably are."

Justin was into men. *Good.*

The front door slammed, and I raised my eyebrows at Nico. "Did you call Marco?" Our older brother was the La Rosa Mafia boss. Nico was the underboss, a title I was happy not to have. Without it, I'd had the freedom to pursue a medical degree, something the family needed, as going to the hospital with a gunshot wound was not ideal.

Nico didn't need to respond. Marco barged in, took the seat to my left, then turned all his focus to me. "Why are you getting involved in anything with Allen Mitchel?"

I shrugged because I couldn't possibly describe how one look at his stepdaughter had resurrected all the feelings from the first time we'd met or that I couldn't say no. It wasn't a normal reaction, and I had no words to make them understand. "He thought offering me a position on the board would sway me."

"What?" An eyebrow arched over one of Marco's green eyes that were so like our mother's.

I already knew what they were both thinking. "It's crazy, I know. I didn't agree to it."

"Wait a minute. It's not a bad idea," Nico said.

"I don't want anything from Allen." I couldn't believe what he was suggesting.

"Of course not. A seat is easy to obtain. There are several

board members that'll vote you in after a well-placed phone call." Nico's chair squeaked in protest as he leaned back.

"But none that I want to control." A flash of dark intent flooded me. "If I did go along with Allen's offer, I would have something on him."

"You would. But that wasn't what I was suggesting." Nico's sat forward. "If you take a position on the board, you can reduce your hours at the hospital. It would be good for the family."

He wasn't wrong. That was part of why I'd gone into medicine in the first place. "Fine. I'll go along with Allen's bribe."

Marco observed me for a minute longer than what made me comfortable. Whatever he saw, he decided to keep it to himself. "Nico and I'll go with you to get the girl."

"No." I couldn't explain it, but I knew it was something I had to do alone. "As far as we know, it's one guy holding her. There's no reason for either of you to go with me."

"We don't know if there are others involved," Marco reasoned. "There's also Guido Amato. His whereabouts are unaccounted for, and he's gunning for you and Luc."

Luc Brambilla was one of the Five Family bosses and had recently married Summer. The longer I debated with my brothers, the more time went by where I could be rescuing Hailey. I needed to appease them somehow and get out of there. "If anything, Guido will go after Luc. And he's on his honeymoon with Summer in Italy. I doubt he's a factor."

"I don't want you going in there alone. If you don't take both of us, then at least have Nico go with."

I met Marco's steady gaze with a determined one of my own. "It's a quiet neighborhood." Nico's footage had only shown one car in the driveway. "Nico can hack the security cameras on the exits of the house and see how many people have entered the house."

"You're being weird about this." Marco cocked his head, and

I didn't like the gleam in his eyes. "Nico can do that, but you'll take security."

"I planned on it." I had to get out of there.

"Wait." Nico opened a desk drawer. "I got this from… someone. Use this if they open a door, or since there aren't any cameras on the side of the house, then get it in through a window."

He handed me a small device that resembled a fly and a controller with a screen that connected to a camera in the fly's eyes. "You're being cagey. Who is the someone you got this from?" I needed the focus off of me, and he was being strange.

Nico shrugged. "A friend in security. No big deal. Anyway, it's a camera, but there isn't audio."

"A fly in January." I grinned. "Should be interesting." It was smart. Flies had ommatidia, made up of thousands of visual receptors. Each one acted as a functioning eye that provided a 360-degree view in its entirety. I wondered if the drone had a 360 camera in it.

"I want security in there with you," Marco insisted.

I held up the tiny drone. "I'll scope out the inside first. They can wait in the car while I do that. If I need them, they'll know. I'll relay what I find out."

"I'll keep digging here. But so far, nothing is coming up on this Justin guy. No excessive debt or anything usual that would be a red flag. And the cameras on the house aren't connected to the internet. I can't hack them."

"It doesn't matter. I'll be careful." I held up the fly again. "Thanks for this and to whoever gave it to you." I winked at Nico as Marco narrowed his gaze on him. There would be no avoiding answering Marco. We could ignore our older brother but not our boss, and a question specific to the equipment fell into the boss category.

I was quickly losing daylight. After we said our goodbyes, I hurried from the house. My car would stick out like a sore thumb. I borrowed keys from one of the guys on our staff. On the way to the loaner car, I grabbed two guards and told them to follow me, adding that they were to be discreet and remain in their vehicle when we got there. They would know if I needed them—they would hear gunshots.

CHAPTER FOUR

TREY

In a nondescript sedan, I headed in the direction Nico had indicated. Forty minutes later, I'd arrived in a low-income subdivision downtown just outside of the city, where each residence looked like a carbon copy of the next. I drove at a moderate pace, looking for anything out of the ordinary. Vehicles lined the streets, some with enough snow on the roofs that I knew they hadn't moved during the day, and others without. All were in front of uniform brick bungalows. I dismissed the homes with the blinds open, searching the area for a white van and a house with all the windows covered.

It wasn't until the middle of the neighborhood that I found the house that matched the address Nico gave me. The blinds were drawn on every window facing the street. Most had at least the second story ones open to let in the fading light. I pulled through the alley, parked two garages away, then got out of the car. The black SUV that had followed pulled behind me as I peeked into the one-car garage's dirty window for the bungalow in question for signs of the van. And there it was. *Got you.*

I motioned for the guards to stay where they were while I

grabbed the tiny drone, its controller, and a hacksaw blade. To avoid the backyard camera above the door, I went in from one house over and approached from the side. Dusk was settling in, which worked in my favor.

I crunched through the thin layer of pristine snow, aware I was leaving a clear trail as I closed in on the house from the side. White paint peeled and flaked from the trim. The dark-red brick appeared tired, same as most houses on the street. It was freezing out, and most people were inside or on their way home from work. A few evergreen bushes lined the side of the house, and I stepped close to a nearby window. The shrubs helped to obscure me as I listened.

When no sounds filtered through my chosen entry point, I put a thin hacksaw blade near the sash lock. When the teeth caught, I pushed then popped it open. After removing the tool, I pried the glass pane up a sliver and set the tiny drone on the sill. A few commands of the control panel launched the pseudoinsect, and I watched on the screen that fed from the fly's eyes, pleased when I saw that it was a 360-degree camera.

The fly flew through what looked like a living room that didn't have any furniture in it then to the dated kitchen. No one was in either of the rooms. I made a sweep of the first floor, noting the coats hanging on hooks on the wall adjacent to the back entrance, one of which looked like it could be Hailey's. *Interesting.* A quick check over the shoes piled below revealed a lone stiletto that looked like the one she'd worn that morning.

Encouraged, I continued the exploration, deciding on the basement rather than the second floor, as the door that led downstairs was open, and a light shone from below. With the fly near the ceiling, I was able to keep it relatively hidden. The stairwell was closed until the bottom quarter, where it opened up without walls and only the railings bracketing the steps.

A few more centimeters, and the view of the lower level was displayed crystal clear on the screen before me. My eyebrows rose at the sight of a man and woman sitting at a small table, a pizza box in front of them, and a video game paused on the TV situated before a large leather sectional. I recognized the woman as Hailey. The man was new to me, but he had to have been Justin—and he fit the visual form of the masked attacker.

Reversing the fly's direction, I did another sweep of the first floor then upstairs. The house was empty except for those two. I returned the fly to the windowsill, shut off the monitor, and pocketed the tiny drone. I set the controller on the hedge, eased the pane up as far as it would go, then climbed inside and pointed my gun in the direction of the basement.

My steps were slow and measured—I didn't want to alert them to any noise from the floor above. It probably wouldn't have mattered, as I could hear the gun noise from the video game they played. In the time it took me to get into position, they must have finished their dinner.

The basement door was in sight, and their voices trickled from below. My ears strained to hear what they were saying. I inched closer, taking care of my steps. Hailey and Justin were partially turned away from where I stood, their bodies angled toward the flat-screen. She looked good—happy—and I noticed a lack of cuts and bruises. I hadn't expected them, but the worry hadn't faded regardless.

Melodic laughter spilled from Hailey's lips, and I froze. There was so much joy in the sound that it filled my soul and lent a lightness that I hadn't realized had been missing. But my life—the Mafia—it took so much, and my residency then establishment at the hospital claimed whatever was left. Not even my sister, Sofia, could extinguish the bleakness that had seeped into me of late, and she was the most capable.

One of them had hit replay on the game, and they argued back and forth good-naturedly. I crept down the remaining steps while they were distracted and facing away. At the bottom,

I eased around the back of the staircase, effectively blocked from their sight by the rear wall of the stairwell.

What was the point of the kidnapping? It was clear they were friends and apparently in it together. The target had to have been Allen, but I couldn't figure out why. As an heiress, Hailey wouldn't need the money. I meant to find out their reasoning behind this without cueing Allen in on what I was doing. I relaxed back into the shadows, content to listen for the time being.

I didn't have a visual from where I stood behind the wall, but their voices carried clearly to where I was. She'd changed from her attire that morning. Instead, she wore a forest-green sweatshirt and, from what I'd seen through the drone's eye, black leggings.

"Gross. How can you can drink that?" Justin said, and I peered around the corner to see the name of the beer Hailey held.

It was an ale. I had to agree with him. I preferred a good IPA or a stout.

"Hey, I don't criticize when you never drink when we go out." She nudged him with her shoulder as they settled onto the couch and resumed their game.

Justin snorted. "You know why."

They were silent for a few seconds while their players entered a battle. When it ended, I strained to hear what Hailey said: "I forgot that alcoholism runs in your family. Sorry about that. This has been a highly stressful day."

"You're telling me." Justin swore, narrowly missing his character getting shot.

"I'm going stir crazy. I need to get out of here."

Justin snorted. "With your one shoe?"

"Just call me freaking Cinderella."

"Funny. The shoe fits—except you have an evil stepfather instead of a stepmother. Well, she is sort of awful too."

"Touché." She lifted her drink in a salute while tapping against the controller with her other hand. "And no stepsiblings, thank God."

As interesting as their conversation was, I didn't plan to wait too much longer before making my presence known.

***

Hailey

I snuck a glance at Justin, not wanting to turn away from the screen and risk my character dying. "You seeing anyone?"

"No one important." He groaned. "You know me. I always pick the wrong guys. I want something serious, and they let me down. Every damn time."

"You and me both." I nudged him with my shoulder, feeling bad for bringing up his love life. "At least you go for it. I'm still dreaming about that guy."

The game froze. He'd paused it then turned to face me, his mouth hanging open. "Still? You know his sister. The guy's not unattainable. You need to go for it."

"Yeah, well." I needed to change the subject fast. The last thing I wanted to get into was how I had it bad for Sofia La Rosa's Mafia boss brother, the man I'd never even met face-to-face. I was such a weirdo. "Hey, we need to put in another call to Allen, up the stakes a little."

"I still can't believe what we did."

"I can't either."

"What are you doing?" Justin paused the game, setting his controller down as he turned toward me, his voice serious.

I didn't want to see the judgment in his eyes, even though he was right to question my motives. I took a deep breath then rested the controller on my crossed legs. After leaning back against the couch,

I turned my head and faced my best friend. We'd known each other since grammar school and had been fast friends since the moment I gave Lucas Davis a bloody nose for shoving Justin to the ground and calling him a terrible slur for gay men on the playground.

Bullies and injustice against those who couldn't defend themselves were my triggers.

Back then, Justin had been a scrawny kid, small for his size and different in how he dressed and acted, an easy target for bullies like Lucas.

My driving force behind why we were hiding in his basement followed the same pattern. Justin had gone along with my crazy scheme without saying a word until now. I shrugged. "I can't let Allen get away with it."

"Do you think your mom will care?" His lips momentarily flattened into a straight line, and I could all but hear the disgust with a dash of pity in his expression.

Pain slashed its sharp claws at my heart. We both knew it. We'd both witnessed how my mom could barely look at me. I should have died, not my sister. We shared the same face, but she had been destined for greatness. I was a disappointment. I didn't know why I bothered to look out for Mom, but I did. Just once, I wished she would see me, realize that I was still alive. It was pointless. Her heart was buried with my sister and her husband, the love of her life.

Tears welled in my eyes, and I brushed them away with an angry swipe of my hands. "It's not for my mom." *It's for me.* To prove to myself I was still there, not Kasey, and that I could make a difference even if it meant taking down my mom's husband in the process. Maybe especially if it meant that—he stole from children.

I knew my sister. She would have been egging me on the whole time while she feigned innocence to our parents. She'd gotten all the acting talent in the family, but I could pull it off.

I'd tapped into Kasey's spirit to perform this morning as if she was whispering in my ear. Part of me believed she had been.

"We don't have to follow through. You could show up back home, looking a mess, and say you were dumped not far from there but blindfolded and told to count to fifty before removing it."

"I get that I went a little over the top with making Allen pay, but I can't let it go. I mean, what the hell did he do with that money, Justin? You know it's not right."

Movement caught my eye, and we both bolted off the couch. I whirled around, heart in my throat and adrenaline coursing through my veins. A man stood by the stairs, casually leaning against the railing.

"What the hell are you doing here!" My fingers went momentarily numb from shock and adrenaline.

Justin's hand found mine, and he tugged lightly. I took a step toward him. I could tell by the way Justin's arm trembled when it brushed against me that he was nervous.

Not me. The sudden surprise at seeing a strange man in the house dissipated when I realized *who* he was. My gaze hungrily crawled over his face. Need coiled in my stomach, and I swore my soul sighed at the sight of him. Traitorous soul—clearly that part of me had forgotten how he'd rejected me.

Trey La Rosa, Sofia's brother, stood there, taking us in. Sofia was a famous fashion designer, and Trey was her favorite brother. I'd seen glimpses of him when I'd grabbed coffee with her, but I'd taken care so that he wouldn't notice me, given how humiliated I'd been after our first encounter that night at the fundraiser.

Sofia and I weren't that close, but whenever I saw her out— getting food or at the boutique—I made a point to chat with her. There wasn't much not to like about Sofia. I longed for an intro to her brother on even footing. But he was a genius, having graduated high school at fifteen then earning a medical degree.

The ransom plan was to extract money that Allen had embezzled, and I'd wondered if Allen would involve Trey. There was no way Allen would risk the police looking further into him. I shoved my out-of-control attraction aside, crossed my arms, and narrowed my eyes at him. I couldn't let him mess with my plan.

CHAPTER FIVE

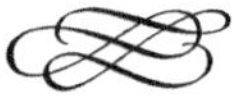

TREY

I leaned against the railing in sight of Hailey and Justin. It only took a moment for her to spot me. She gasped then jumped to her feet and whirled around. Justin's reaction mirrored hers, but he was half a second behind. I kept my gun pointed at the ground, as I hadn't seen any weapons on them or in the room. Didn't mean they didn't have any, but I wasn't worried. Justin grabbed Hailey's forearm and tugged her close.

"What do you want?" Justin's voice shook, the fear on his face mixing with recognition.

Hailey wrenched herself free of his arm, her gemstone-green eyes flashing fire. "I know who you are and where you work, Trey La Rosa."

Of course you do. I grinned, letting them see the malice behind it. I wasn't in the mood for games. "Who else is involved in your little scheme?"

Justin tightly closed his mouth as his gaze narrowed, but it was Hailey who responded. "Allen sent you?" She snorted, showing not an ounce of fear. "Figures he would have someone else do his dirty work for him. But what doesn't make sense is why a doctor would have a gun."

"Surely, you know who I am." I kept my voice low, pushing off the railing and closing the distance between us. I stopped before Justin. A sheen of sweat coated his upper lip. "You must have heard the rumors." I grabbed Hailey's arm and eased her away from him. Justin remained frozen in front of me. "I'm guessing no one knows of your involvement?"

He shook his head, his pupils narrowing to pinpricks, a common response to fear. Hailey struggled, but I pulled her against my side then pointed my gun at Justin. She stilled in my grasp.

"We aren't going to have a problem here, are we?"

A shaky "no" left his mouth as I backed away with Hailey in tow.

"Call the cops or anyone else, and she'll pay for it. Understand?"

Justin looked ready to piss himself but nodded. I grasped Hailey's arm and pulled her with me up the stairs, the gun trained on Justin as we went. As soon as we were on the first floor, she tried to yank her arm away, but I refused to release her.

"You won't get away with this." Her green eyes flashed, and a pretty shade of pink settled on her high cheekbones.

I couldn't remember the last time I'd had so much fun. I holstered my gun. "Who do you think Justin will call?" Amusement laced my words as I lifted her through the window then climbed through after her before she had a chance to run off. A bitter wind whipped through the breezeway between the two houses. A full-body shiver wracked her body, and I bent then positioned her in a fireman's carry over my shoulder. She didn't have a jacket or shoes on, just fuzzy socks that were wet from the snow. As she sputtered behind me, her small fists hitting my back, I exited through the neighbor's yard then to the alleyway, keeping out of range of the camera he had set up for the backyard before I placed her on her feet next to the car I'd borrowed.

Her wavy hair tangled in front of her face, and I wanted to push the silky strands away to see the fire reflected in her gaze. "He'll call the police."

I snorted then crowded her, giving her no choice but to get into the passenger side of my car. I bent so that we were at eye level before shutting the door. "Take note of the armed guards in the vehicle behind us. They won't let you get away while I'm rounding the car to get in."

Once she was inside, I ran her seat belt across her then clicked it into place. After shutting the door, I went around the front then got into my seat and started the car. Without the headlights to avoid notice until we passed a few houses, we pulled out slowly to avoid attracting attention.

"We both know he won't call the cops. What's he going to say? He was holding you hostage, but I took you from him? And even if he calls in a tip that he saw me with you, it won't matter." We had the chief of police in our pocket, but that wasn't information I was going to share. I weaved through the streets, uncaring of my speed, and closed in on the entrance to the highway.

"Where are you taking me?"

"Funny how your little plan backfired." I laughed and floored it as we merged onto the highway and headed toward my lake-front house. My body thrummed with electricity from touching her. For the second time since Teresa died, I felt like I was alive, and I didn't want that to end.

I was taking her to my place in the city. What she and Justin had concocted intrigued me too much to expose them for the liars they were to Allen. The ride was quiet, and I let her sit with her thoughts. I could only imagine what was running through her head. After witnessing the little scene in the basement, she was obviously rebelling and taking her stepfather for a run for his money.

When we arrived at the underground entrance to my greystone across from Lake Michigan and off Lake Shore Drive, I rolled down my window and motioned for the guards to leave. I did not need them, as I had my own men monitoring the perimeter. They waited until we passed the gated entry before pulling away.

Once we were parked, I got out of the car and opened her door. Sam, the head of my guards, approached, and I told him to have someone take the loaner car back and return with my Maserati.

I led her to the elevator with a firm but gentle grasp on her arm. We rode it to the top. The doors parted with a soft swoosh into my living room. The kitchen was to the left, and a fireplace was situated across from a large sectional to our right. Directly before us were floor-to-ceiling windows and an accordion glass slider with a stunning view of the lake. It was my favorite part of my home. My sister, Sofia, had worked with an interior designer and decorated it in a way she knew I would like with dusty blue-gray and natural stone. I loved it, and for some strange reason, I wanted Hailey to like it too.

Hailey stood between the kitchen and living room, her gaze trained on the water. I released her and went to grab a bottle of wine and two glasses. I couldn't have cared less if she had any, but I needed it after my shift at the hospital. Once I was on the board, I would cut my hours drastically. I didn't have even the small amount of time off that a typical ER surgeon had, given my obligation to family.

The sound of the cork's extraction must have pulled Hailey from her thoughts, and she turned in my direction with wide eyes. I couldn't help but smirk. I motioned for her to join me, nudging one of the wineglasses to the opposite side of the island, closer to her. With measured steps, she inched over. Her trepidation was in direct conflict with her earlier bravado.

I waited for her to take a sip before I got down to business. "There are a few things you need to be aware of—there is no escaping. Even if you managed to take the elevator to the garage, guards will stop you."

The spunk from earlier returned, and the corner of her mouth quirked up. "You'll have to leave at some point. There are other ways I can get help."

"Your purse, coat, and shoes are back at Justin's. So no phone. There isn't a landline in here for you to access. You won't be able to break my password to send an email." I held up my hand to stop her protest. "And even if you do manage to scream from the penthouse balcony, no one will hear you. The front of this building and those on either side have construction and detours set up for anyone who tries to walk even close to the perimeter. No one will hear you."

"You're forgetting one major factor—Justin."

"And what do you think he's going to do? I'm aware he's your friend. We've already discussed the police situation and how even if he went to report that I had you, nothing would be done."

"Justin will find a way." She lifted her glass in a silent toast to my downfall. "And when he does, I'll be laughing all the way to the door while they drag you away in handcuffs."

I took a sip of my wine, held her gaze, and didn't say a word. A few minutes passed while we simply drank and sized each other up. Her fingers toyed with the glass stem. I didn't want to argue with her about her friend.

"Why did Allen send you?" She squared her shoulders aggressively and adopted a commanding voice.

Brave. Not once had she cowered, and I secretly loved every second of her strength. But it only heightened the attraction I had for her, something I would have to be very careful to keep in check. "Why?" That was an excellent question, considering that her stunt reeked of rebellion and a lack of a healthy relationship between the two. "The only answer I can come up with is that the ransom demand said no cops. Maybe he cared enough that he didn't want you delivered to him in pieces. Nice touch with that threat, by the way."

The corners of her lips twitched, but she schooled her features before giving in to the emotion entirely. My gaze dropped to her full lower lip, and I wondered how she would react if I ran my tongue over it then tugged it between my teeth before exploring her mouth until she clung to me, begging for more. I pushed off the back counter where I had been leaning to shift so that I stood at the island, hiding my arousal from view. That was going to be a problem.

"You won't know for sure what happened this morning. Maybe I got away? Or the kidnapper wasn't there when you broke into Justin's house?"

"I saw the security tapes. One person in the van happened to fit Justin's height and build. So cut the crap. What are your plans for the money? I can't imagine you're hurting for cash, based on who your mother is."

"Why do you want to know?" She tilted her head to the side, a mass of curls tumbling over her shoulder. I wanted to thread my fingers through it and see if the strands would curl around them. Would they be as silky as they looked?

I closed my eyes briefly, working hard to get myself under control. It had to have been the long hours I'd put in lately. I was tired. That had to be the reason for my response to her. "I know your mother and what she's worth. Not only that, but I know how much you have in your trust fund to the penny. So I'll ask again. What did you hope to gain by ransoming the money from Allen? Was it a stunt to get his attention?"

Her head jerked back. "How old do you think I am?"

"Twenty-two. Dropped out of MIT after a year and a half, and you haven't done anything with your life other than hang out with your best friend and play video games in his basement."

An angry flush darkened her cheeks. "I see you've been

talking to my mom. You're not the only one. I've spoken with Sofia, and I know all about what you do, what family you come from."

"Then you're aware that provoking me isn't a good option." I wasn't getting the information from her that I needed, but I was sure as hell enjoying sparring with her.

She shrugged then took a sip of her wine. When she set it down, a slow smile curved her lips. "You may be Mafia, but you're a doctor, and you've sworn an oath."

I laughed. "That's naïve of you. I might save people, but I also kill them." I put my drink down, fatigue clouding the edges of my vision. Caffeine was a better option, and I pivoted to where the Nespresso machine sat on the coffee bar that Sofia had insisted upon.

I was glad my sister had taken charge of getting my space in order. I used it as a place to crash after long residency hours, but she'd barged in and announced she was decorating it. We were the closest of our siblings, and I never took her for granted. When Ivan, our Russian mob nemesis, tortured her, it had been some of the darkest moments of my life.

I'd been up for forty-eight hours straight between the hospital shifts and researching Hailey. Soon, I would crash. I had about two hours tops before that happened, and I needed to get to a place with her where I wasn't worried she would kill me in my sleep.

"Why didn't you finish at MIT? It's a great school."

Silence hung heavily between us until she pushed out a breath. "I was bored. I guess I lacked purpose there. I was skipping classes and partying too much, and the major I was in just didn't seem like a good fit."

"Why didn't you change majors?" I took a large gulp of coffee, praying the caffeine would do its thing.

She snorted. "Okay, boy genius. We're not all wired like you, knowing what to do with the rest of our lives."

I chuckled at her ridiculous nickname. "Lots of people don't know what they want to major in or even what career to choose. But giving up... it seems like a waste unless you're committed to being a socialite like your mother."

"Yeah, no." She gestured to her high-end yoga pants and sweatshirt—which I only knew were designer because my sister had a similar outfit. "That's not me."

"Tell me why you did it?"

Her brows furrowed. "Drop out of college? We've been over that."

"Faked the abduction," I clarified. She worried her lower lip, and I had to fight from fixating on how soft it looked.

As she parted her lips to finally tell me what her reason was, my phone rang. I was on call and had to answer it. She snapped her mouth shut, probably happy for the reprieve. Sandy's voice came through the speaker, letting me know that Katherine had checked out and my parents had taken her with them to our jet, which would fly them to Italy.

CHAPTER SIX

HAILEY

I couldn't look away from Trey. With his phone pressed to his ear, his gaze locked on me. He thanked whomever it was then disconnected the call, a slow, calculating smile curving his lips. The intensity was staggering. So many emotions bombarded me, and I wasn't sure if I wanted to run to him or away. My nerves kicked into high gear as if he could see into me. I was leaning toward running away.

"What was the money going to be used for?"

"The children's cancer wing," I blurted. I didn't know whether I told him out of fear of whatever that look he had on his face meant or if I was in shock from the day's events. *What just happened?*

"Huh, okay." He eased back. "I'm on board with that."

"Really?" I couldn't believe it. I rubbed my eyes then blinked a few times. I'd never thought things would go that way. But maybe I shouldn't have been surprised. Sofia always spoke highly of Trey, and blackmailing someone wasn't above him—he was Mafia, after all.

But I was still wary of him. He had rejected me, after all.

He chugged the rest of his coffee, and I couldn't help but

notice the deep circles under his eyes. My plan to find a way out of the mess wavered. "What will you get out of this deal?"

"A position on the board." He pushed the mug aside and leaned his elbows on the island.

"Why do you need Allen for that?" I couldn't believe he didn't have other contacts who would give him a spot.

Trey chuckled. "I don't. But can you imagine him having to sponsor me for a chair?"

I wasn't following. "So you took on his crisis rather than tell him to shove it? He could have gone to the cops. I don't understand why you got involved. It seems like this is more of a headache for you."

"It isn't. I couldn't pass up a chance to make Allen squirm. And the interesting part was when he said he couldn't involve the police further was because of his fear of the repercussions if he didn't meet the ransom demand. I didn't buy it. Plus, he hates me. I guessed that he was hiding something, and I suspected you were too."

That surprised me, momentarily distracting me from how close he was and from the way his eyes seemed to reach the deepest part of my soul. My pulse kicked up a notch. His nearness made my train of thought waver and I blurted out my last thought before it was gone. "Why did you think I was hiding something? You said you saw the recording of when I was snatched in front of the hospital and Allen."

"It was a tiny moment before you were tossed into the van. You hesitated. There was no one else on camera helping your attacker."

"He could have said something threatening to cause me to stop struggling."

"That was a possibility. Tell me the real reason you staged your abduction and went after Allen. Why him?"

Telling Trey hadn't required much thought. He was still going along with my fake hostage situation and the ransom demand. "Mom gave Allen a large check to help fund the children's cancer wing. I was there when she did it and got too excited. It was weird, so I followed the money trail. Imagine my surprise when there were no new deposits into the children's donations."

"You hacked into the hospital records?"

"Yeah." I didn't worry about him turning me in. "And Allen's. The money didn't show up in any of his accounts."

"Are you still looking for where it went?"

"I am." And when I found it, I would nail that fucker to the wall. It was bad enough he was with Mom—why I defended her when she didn't even like me was annoying—but to steal from kids… finally, I would have proof of just how much of a scumbag he was.

"Well, at least we know where you're putting your MIT skills to use."

I laughed. He had me there. "The problem is that my computer is at Justin's." I needed it to look for where Allen was hiding the money.

"I'll pick one up for you later." He topped off my wine. "We need to come to an understanding about your stay here."

After a hearty gulp of my drink, I got ready to negotiate with a criminal. Geesh. I couldn't call him that because I was one, too, given the things I'd been pulling lately. "You'll help me with the fake ransom, and the full amount will go to the children's wing and not in your pocket?"

"Hailey, I do not need the money. I'm also curious why Allen is stealing from kids."

It could be an even better plan than the one I have with Justin. "We're partners in this? You get the money from him while I figure out what he did with it in the first place?"

"We are." He reached across the island, extending his hand.

His large palm swallowed mine, and a jolt of electricity traveled from where we touched along my arm, sending shock waves through my synapses. I pulled my hand back quickly, fighting the full-body-shiver effect he had on me. "Deal."

"There are rules I'll expect you to abide by. No leaving the building unless I'm with you." He waited for me to nod my agreement. "And no contacting anyone while we're in negotiations with Allen. That includes Justin."

"I'm not okay with not talking to Justin."

"I'll amend that one—no telling Justin where you are."

"Sure."

"One of my guards will head up here in a few minutes. Added security until we reach a level of trust."

Okay... I hopped off the chair and went to the fridge, pausing with my hand on the door. "Do you mind if I make something to eat?"

He ran his hand over his face then shook his head. "Help yourself. I need to crash for a little while. There are two spare bedrooms. Pick the one you want to use. If you need something, just pound on the door to my room. Remote for the TV is on the coffee table."

As he walked toward the living room then disappeared down a hallway, I pulled out sandwich ingredients. He said he would get me a computer, but I could kick back and watch a couple of movies in the meantime.

Trey might have preferred that I not contact Justin, but I probably would. It was only fair that I let my best friend and partner in crime know that I was safe.

I plopped down on the buttery leather couch with my plate and a large glass of water. I liked the wine but wasn't in the mood for it. I channel surfed for a while then ended up settling for a rom-com. I needed something funny and sweet with a happily ever after—my kryptonite. My sister, Kasey, and I used to swoon over those kinds of movies, and to be honest, I still did, even though that type of ending wasn't in the cards for me. My last boyfriend had emphasized that when he ended things.

One of Trey's security guys stepped off the elevator, but I didn't pay him any attention, and soon, he blended into the surroundings so that it was easy to forget he was even there.

Pushing everything from my mind, I let myself enjoy the movie because soon, I would have to choose one of the bedrooms to sleep in while trying to ignore the fact that the man I was wildly attracted to slept only a few feet away.

CHAPTER SEVEN

TREY

I slept like the dead after being up for so long. The smell of coffee wafting under my bedroom door was what drew me to the kitchen. Only, it wasn't Hailey but my sister sitting on my couch, her leather boots kicked up on the table. I trudged over to her, blinking a few times to clear the last remnants of sleep so that I could deal with how cheery she seemed. *Hailey must still be sleeping.*

I nodded at the guard who'd watched over Hailey while I'd crashed last night. After an update, I dismissed him and turned to my sister.

"Brother dearest," Sofia said with a grin. "One of the guards mentioned you had a guest. He tried to discourage me from coming up here, but I twisted his arm, and we came to an understanding."

"Which guard?" All my men knew to let her up and that my sister would always have access to my home, but if they ran their mouths, that would be a problem.

"He's new, and I saw your captain heading over to him." She waved my concern away. "I'm sure he'll have his head on straight before I leave."

"Why are you here?" I dropped onto the couch next to her and took the to-go cup she handed me. I was just harassing her —I almost always wanted Sofia around. She was my favorite and understood me on a level that even our brothers didn't. I took a sip of coffee, letting the first hit of caffeine flood my body.

Sof grabbed her mane of wavy chestnut hair and swept it to one side. "Enzo had a meeting with Marco and the other bosses today. I missed you."

I leaned against the couch, debating whether I should go back to bed for another few hours. Sof smacked my stomach, and I grunted then forced myself to pick up my head to glare at her.

"So who do you have here? Anyone I know?"

I grinned because she would get a laugh out of the situation I was in. "Hailey Carmichael."

She gave colorful commentary as I explained. We could have been twins for how in tune we were and how much we thought alike.

"What? No way." Sofia grinned. "I love her."

"How well do you know her?" I knew they'd had coffee together from what Sofia had said when I first met Hailey at the fundraiser. Sofia had taken Hailey under her wing after I'd walked away when the Coffee Stop was mentioned, but I didn't know if they were actual friends or just acquaintances.

"Well enough. We met in the boutique"—she pursed her lips —"maybe a year ago? I can't remember. There was a period of time we didn't talk, but that was when everything was going down with Ivan, and Enzo took me to Italy for Fashion Week."

"Not helpful." I downed the rest of my coffee then noticed a white pastry box on the kitchen island. I got up, retrieved it, settled back on the couch, and flipped the lid open. My mouth watered at the assortment of pastries from the Italian bakery we loved. When I reached for the cream puff with chocolate shavings sprinkled on top, she smacked my hand.

"That's mine."

I laughed because there was no crossing Sof when she set her mind to something. Leaving her pasty alone, I grabbed a *sfogliatella* then bit into it, groaning as I chewed. The pastry was like a little window into Italy, and I was ready to visit for a while. She nudged my shoulder. She understood—it was from our all-time favorite bakery in the States. Then she took her cream puff, and we ate in silence.

"Hailey's different from most of the rich kids who went to university."

"She didn't go to the same college as us," Sofia pointed out.

"Not the point, smartass. Even though her family is loaded, you would never know she came from money. I don't know her that well, but I always have fun when we hang out. She's never gotten deep with me. I did learn a little about her family, though. Her sister was killed in a car accident with their biological father when she was in middle school. Her mom never recovered, and I got the impression they have a strained relationship."

"And she doesn't get along with her mom's husband," I added.

"Bingo." Sofia took another sip of her latte. "I think you'll like her."

"I do. We're in a screw-over-Allen plot together." I tapped my empty to-go coffee with hers.

"Yeah, that's not what I meant."

"Listen, matchmaker, I don't have the energy or time to date anyone right now."

"It's been months since Teresa died. You need to get back out there. And I think when you do, you'll realize that your feelings for her weren't as deep as you'd thought."

"Sof"—my head fell back against the couch, and I turned toward her—"drop it."

She smiled, but it was sad, lacking her usual infectious charming. "You know I love you."

I tugged her into my arms and squeezed. "I know. I love you, too, weirdo."

She snorted then shoved me away. "I've got to run. People to annoy—mainly my husband."

I stood with her. "I don't think there's anything you can do that would annoy him. You've got Enzo wrapped around your little finger."

"Goes both ways, brother dearest. I'll catch up with you later." She winked. "Have fun with Hailey."

As soon as the elevators closed behind my sister, I heard another door open. I needed more coffee. I started one mug at the Nespresso machine and took down another to make Hailey some.

"Whoa, what's this?"

I half turned to answer her. She stood on the other side of the couch in her leggings and a tight and very thin spaghetti-strap shirt. No bra. Anything I was about to say died in my mouth as my gaze slowly crawled over her, beginning at the top of her messy bedhead waves, down to gorgeous face, and then over her lithe body. She wasn't overly curvy but had the type of build I was a sucker for—a cross between a gymnast and a dancer.

She ignored my staring as she lifted the box and gave it a gentle shake. "Can I have one?"

I shook my head, breaking the spell. "Yeah, help yourself. Coffee's ready." I turned and grabbed both mugs then got creamer out of the fridge and set it next to hers. I needed mine full strength and black. "Do you want creamer in your coffee?"

"Yes, thanks."

It was going to be more challenging than I'd thought to have her in my personal space. She brought a glazed doughnut over to the island and climbed onto one of the chairs. Off in the distance, the vastness of the lake stretched for as far as the eye could see, creating a sense of peace in the penthouse despite my raging emotions for my temporary houseguest.

"Are you on shift today?" Her green eyes met mine as she took a bite of her pastry.

"No. I have the next few days off." I needed it. Between my family and the hospital hours, something had to give, hence my desire to be on the board. I wanted to stay involved but not as much in the daily grind.

"Great. I need clothes."

I grunted. Sofia had just been there—I could have asked her to help. "We can't go to your mom's house, which I know is where you're living. My sister can bring some by."

She rolled her eyes. "I love Sofia, but I'm perfectly capable of shopping for clothes myself. Plus, I know Allen's schedule. He won't be around when I go."

I mulled over her reasoning. She had a point. My gaze wandered over her shoulders and perky breasts before snapping back to her face. It was going to be a long week. "If you won't let Sofia handle it, then I'm going with you. There's no telling if Allen hired someone to attempt to recover you."

A smirk curved her lips. "Aside from you?"

"Okay, smart-ass." I put my coffee mug in the dishwasher then headed toward my room. "I'm going to grab a shower. Then we're out of here."

Hailey

I tapped my nails against the island, debating over another pastry as Trey's phone rang. Not even a minute later, he appeared, wearing a strained expression. A sliver of alarm went through me. "Is everything all right?"

He ran a hand through his hair, disheveling the dark strands on top. "I have to go to the hospital. A patient I treated took a turn for the worse and needs immediate surgery." He glanced at his watch. "If the operation goes well, I should be back here close to dinner."

"I understand." I got up to make a second cup of coffee. *What the heck am I going to do for an entire day?*

"I'll have Sam—he's the captain of my security team—get a phone for you with my number programmed into it and his, in case you need anything that isn't here. Nico will have a computer for you, too, eventually." He paused on his way to the elevator. "Sam will order lunch for you. Tell him what you want when he brings the phone up."

I leaned a hip against the counter as he grabbed a coat then rushed into the elevator. As I glanced around the open floor plan, a sense of panic bubbled at the prospect of having nothing to do. There were no video games. Until his guard brought the new phone, I didn't have my Kindle app, so reading was also out of the question. I could entertain myself if I had a computer, but I didn't even have that.

After a quick shower, I decided more coffee was in order. Once the machine stopped spitting out my morning drug of choice, I added creamer then went over to one of the swiveling club chairs closest to the balcony. It was so quiet inside. I wished it wasn't winter so I could open the glass sliders and listen to the sound of the waves. Content to stare at the water for the time being, I sipped my coffee and waited for Sam to bring me a phone.

Fifteen minutes later, the elevator doors opened to reveal a towering man stacked with muscle and dressed all in black. I tensed at the invasion even though I was expecting him. "Are you Sam?"

He grinned, flashing a deep dimple on his left cheek. "I am. Boss wanted me to bring you a phone and find out where to get your lunch from."

"Thanks." I greedily accepted the new iPhone. "Um, lunch…" I rattled off a place I guessed wouldn't be too far from there for a sandwich and salad. I honestly just wanted him to go so I could call Justin.

As soon as he left, my fingers flew over the keypad. Good thing I had his number memorized. It rang three times. *Pick up.*

"Hello?" Justin's voice had a tentative edge.

"Justin! It's me." I curled my feet under me and couldn't help smiling.

"Hailey? Oh my God, I've been so worried. I almost went to the police."

I tensed. "Don't. I promise you I'm completely fine. Trey is helping us."

"Girl, I think you're brainwashed." I could practically see his hip cocked and the eye roll that he only flashed in times of complete annoyance with my antics. "Don't forget I know you're his biggest stalker."

My gaze darted around as if Trey was within hearing distance. "I am not."

"Um-hm, I saw the drool in the corner of your mouth when he showed up in my basement."

Heat infused my cheeks. He wasn't wrong. "You think he's hot too."

"Hails, I would have to be blind not to. Tell me what's going on. Did you sleep with him?"

"You're insane. And the answer is no." Not that I hadn't thought about it.

"I'm disappointed. Tell me everything—and it better not be

that you're in the friend zone, which is likely since you haven't slept with him."

I was not addressing that. "Things are honestly going well. I told him why we did it, and he said he would help get the money from Allen and have it allocated to the children's donations."

"When you say help, what do you mean?" Justin's voice sounded strange, tense. "Is he going to hurt Allen?"

"No. Nothing like that." I dropped a leg and swiveled the chair from side to side while we talked. "Allen doesn't even know he has me. We're just playing out the ransom demands like normal. And on that note, I'll need you to call him with that voice-altering thing in two days and tell him where the drop is. Trey will pick it up then give it to me."

"Do you trust him?" Someone asked a question in the background, and Justin muffled the phone, but his voice still came through. "Amelia, I'm busy. Go ask Chris for a lead." There was a pause, and I had to stifle my laughter. He and Amelia were work frenemies. "Shoo."

There was a rustling noise then the sound of a door closing before he huffed. "I cannot believe she asked me about the research I did the other day."

Unable to hold it in any longer, I laughed loudly. Justin worked at a financial magazine. It wasn't his dream job, as he was an assistant to one of the lead reporters, but as he said, it paid the bills. Amelia reported to one of the other people in charge, and they sort of jockeyed for whatever their bosses needed, which was sometimes closely related.

"Drama aside"—I was referring to Justin, and we knew it—"I do trust Trey. He doesn't like Allen, and we both know he doesn't have a shortage of funds. Besides, he's a doctor. Why wouldn't he be on board to help?"

There was a long pause, and I pulled at a loose thread at the bottom of my shirt.

"I'm worried about you, Hails."

"I promise, I'm fine."

"That's debatable." His voice was infused with the teasing quality innate to his nature. "You must smell rank with only the one outfit. Did he run away screaming yet?"

"*Pfff*. Shows what you know. We were going to go shopping for clothes, but he got called into the hospital for emergency surgery."

"It was the clothes, wasn't it? He made that up. Come on, you can tell me."

"You're lucky I'm not anywhere near you." I would have cracked him upside the head for that one. Not too hard, of course.

"I can feel the back of my head stinging as if you were." The sound of a keyboard filtered through, and I could imagine him sitting at his desk and typing an email. "If he's not around, let's meet for lunch."

"I wish I could, but I'm sort of under house arrest. And don't say anything! Your mind is always in the gutter."

Justin's throaty chuckle filled my ears. "You love that about me."

"Sadly, I do."

"I've got to run. Duty calls at this hellhole and I need to pay my mortgage."

"Still haven't met your dream sugar daddy?"

"Don't I wish. If you find anyone, put in a good word for me?"

"Miss you." I didn't want to keep him on the phone at work.

He made a kissing sound then disconnected the call. *Now, what am I going to do?* It was as good a time as any to binge Netflix. I got up, rinsed my coffee mug, then put it in the dishwasher. I grabbed the remote, hit the power button, and got comfortable in front of the TV. As I clicked through the movies and series I could watch, I had a strange feeling of what it would be like if I lived with Trey and how easily I could see myself doing that.

The only problem was that anytime I thought things were going well, they blew up in my face. I couldn't help but worry about what disaster was headed my way.

CHAPTER EIGHT

HAILEY

I jolted awake when Trey sat next to me on the leather couch, and I swore I could hear my heart kick into overdrive. I blinked the room back into focus. I must have fallen asleep bingeing Netflix and waiting for him to come back from the hospital. He grinned at me, and I swore he was even sexier in person than in the pictures. Justin and I had dished about our dream guys, and he was mine. *But really, who wouldn't like a hot doctor with a bad boy side? Sign me up!*

If only. I had to laugh at myself. We were together under the weirdest circumstances. He'd hijacked my ransom situation. I never would have thought that Trey La Rosa would break in to Justin's house and whisk me away to his.

I was romanticizing it, but it felt good. I sank my teeth into my bottom lip to prevent myself from saying anything stupid. I wished I could run off to the bathroom and make a quick call to my best friend. After he got over the fear of a smokin' hot Mafia guy breaking into his house, he would have to admit that Trey was fine. *Ah—get a grip!*

"Did the operation go okay?"

"It did. He's in recovery and doing well. The doctor on call today is monitoring him, so I should be good. Let's hope." He rested his head against the couch, and I noticed the dark circles under his eyes again. "So, we've got three days that you'll need to hide out?"

That shocked me back to reality. "O-oh"—*damn it, Hailey, stop stuttering.* "Yep. Allen is supposed to hand over the cash then."

"Why cash? Why not have him transfer the funds directly into the donation account?"

"That would be the logical thing to do." I tucked my unruly hair behind my ear. "Allen knows how I feel about the children's wing and fundraising. The first thing he would think if that was the ransom demand was that I was orchestrating it."

"Which you are." A smile played around the corners of Trey's lips, and I grinned too.

"Yeah, but the goal was to keep him from figuring that out, not to lead him to who was behind everything."

"I haven't had a day off in a while." He picked up the remote from the coffee table and flipped it in his hand. "I'm not even sure what to do. Got any ideas?"

I glanced around the open space, again noting the lack of video games. Disappointing. The kitchen caught my eye. "What about making drinks and sitting on the balcony?" I pointed to a small electronic firepit. "You've got a source of heat out there."

He grinned. "It's January. That won't help even a little. We could get the fire going in here."

I smirked. "You mean by flicking the switch?" I'd already noted it was an electric one.

He chuckled. "City living. It's not like I have time to chop wood. Nor do I want to deal with ordering and stocking it. That's a lot easier."

I shook my head. "I want to say I'm disappointed, but I prefer the convenience of electric too." I got to my feet, headed into the kitchen, then opened a cabinet before going in search of other types of alcohol. When I found where he kept his liquor, I pulled out the rum and a few other bottles.

"Whoa, what are you planning on making?" Trey was by my side, rummaging around in the fridge. He took out a charcuterie board and set it on the counter.

I stopped and stared. "Why do you have a ready-made meat-and-cheese board?"

"Sofia." He shrugged. "She brought it over with the pastries. No idea why, but I'm not complaining." Eyeing the alcohol bottles lined up on the counter, he took out the orange juice. "If you're leaning toward tropical drinks, there's some small cans of pineapple juice and some other mixers over there." He pointed to the pantry to the left of the fridge.

"I was thinking rum runners, Caribbean style." I thought that was what they were called the last time I had them in the tropics. No one made them as they did there, and I would never order one in the States. If only we were beachside. "Or maybe piña coladas." I could suck those down just as dangerously.

"Where do you go in the Caribbean?" He pulled a fancy blender out of the pantry, set it on the island, then got a cupful of ice and added it. *I guess we're starting with piña coladas.*

"Where wouldn't I go? Well, scratch that. There are a few places." A pang of longing hit me. "My sister and I made our parents take us a few times a year when we were teenagers."

"She was a year older than you?"

He knew. I didn't know if that made it worse or better. Kasey would have been all over him if she had been there. God, I missed her. "Kasey was everything I'm not. Beautiful, outgoing, and talented. She wanted to be an actress, and she was crazy good. My parents adored her. It didn't matter to me, though. We were close." The splash of pineapple then coconut juice into the blender drew my focus, and I tried to push aside the ache of her absence. It never fully went away. "Justin was one of the only friends we had in common."

He flipped the switch, and the blender whirled to life. He poured the concoction into two tall glasses then added reusable straws when it was done. The first sip was heaven. I closed my eyes and could imagine my toes in the sand and the sun warming my skin. The sound of the ocean rolling and crashing against the shore played from memory as the taste of the drink coated my mouth. "This is good."

He winked then took a long draw on his straw. When he came up for air, he grimaced. "I'm not going to be able to have more of these without feeling sick. Let's switch to rum runners after."

I shrugged. I loved them both, and I got it. He probably drank hard liquor or wine, maybe even beer. Sugary drinks had the potential to mess with one's stomach, for sure. I moved to the other side of the island and climbed onto a seat, pulling the charcuterie board closer so I could snag a piece of cheese.

"It had to be difficult after she died." He wasn't letting it go, and I sighed, resigned to the conversation. "If one of my siblings were killed, I think I'd go on a rampage."

"I did, but in my way." *By hibernating.* "I swore I could see her everywhere, even hear her voice. I felt like I was going crazy. When she wasn't talking in my head, it felt like losing her all over again. Then I would simply exist, curled in a ball and hidden under my covers. Sometimes, days would go by. The staff brought me food. I survived, even if my mom didn't check on me once. She was mourning, too, but we should have relied on each other. Instead, she shut me out." I downed half the drink, not even tasting it.

The shaved ice numbed my mouth and my brain enough to shut me up. I shivered, the silence I'd lived with since Kasey and Dad died sinking into me with the memory of that time. *Why am I spilling all this to him?* I hadn't even told Justin everything—like how my mom ignored me back then. Still did, in fact. Other than Justin, I was completely and utterly alone.

Mom's focus had always been on my sister. It hadn't bothered me then. I had Dad and Kasey's attention. And Mom was dramatic—which was likely the main reason she had such a close relationship with Kasey.

I shook off the abyss of loneliness, pasted on an I'm-okay expression, then raised my head and faced him.

He stood across from me, a deep-seated rage simmering in his cognac eyes. "Family doesn't always do what's best."

With a wave of my hand, I brushed his words away. Setting the drink down with only a few sips left, I wracked my brain on how to take the focus off of my past. "Sofia's great. I haven't met your brothers, though." The last of the anger seemed to drain away as he went with my conversation shift.

"She's a handful, but that's one of the things I love about her." He chuckled. "If you only knew her when she was younger. She'd be right there with the rest of us, playing war in the backyard or video games inside, usually because I'd want her there— we're closest in age. But mess with her clothes in any way, and it was like a holy terror was unleashed."

"I can see that." I grinned. "I saw her once when she noticed a stain on her shirt, and the range of emotions that flitted across her face frightened me. I realized then and there never to spill anything on her." I knew from talking with her that the brothers all shared her same quick fuse if anyone they cared about was threatened.

"Sofia takes after Mom with her love of fashion, but the temper... I don't know where that comes from. As for my brothers, I have a feeling you'll meet them soon. Marco took over the position of Mafia boss since my father retired. And Nico has a few things in common with you."

My eyebrows raised. "Really? So he lacks direction too?"

He frowned. "You don't lack direction, Hailey. Stop being so hard on yourself. Not figuring out what you wanted to do in college isn't unusual or a big deal. Many people struggle with what they want to do with the rest of their lives. Having all the answers at a young age isn't common."

"But you did."

"Stop." Trey's gaze narrowed. "I grew up in a different world, and it shaped me and what I saw myself doing in the future. Plus, my brain is wired to figure things out. It comes naturally to me. But my family—there was a time when we almost lost Dad from a gunshot wound. It left a lasting impression. Violence is commonplace. We learned to view each day as a gift because it could be our last. The thought of anything happening to the ones I love was what pointed me in the direction of medicine. I wanted to be able to save them if I could. The decision was for purely selfish reasons."

"Wow. Did you hear yourself? Being a doctor is never a selfish occupation. You're caring for others." I shook my head then lifted my glass and finished the last sip. He got up and mixed a pitcher of rum runners with orange juice, a few different varieties of alcohol, and nutmeg—per my abridged recipe—then poured some into two glasses. I accepted the new drink with enthusiasm. "Thank you."

"Let's take this into the other room." He carried the pitcher, the food, and his drink. Once in the family room, he set them on the live-edge coffee table before turning on the fireplace with the flick of a switch.

The lighting was dim and comforting, and I sank into the couch, my drink in hand and going down far too quickly. I needed to pace myself. "Do you see yourself working at the hospital long-term?"

He leaned back, and his black button-down shirt stretched tightly across his broad shoulders, highlighting the muscle underneath the fabric. *What would it feel like to be held in his embrace rather than a mere touch?* I inhaled sharply through my nose. I couldn't keep fantasizing about him. This situation wasn't what I'd daydreamed about in the past. We were simply working together to stop Allen from cheating kids in need. I was only there because we had a partnership—an agreement—and I had to stay hidden until the ransom was paid.

"No. I enjoy working there, but my family needs me. I'm getting the experience necessary in surgery and the ER for now. Having a seat on the board will keep me in the loop with changes in the field, and I'll work on select cases. At least, that's my current plan."

"What will you do once you're on the board—about Allen, I mean?" There was no love lost between the two, and I wondered whether he would get Allen kicked off or change his position in the hospital. I was all for it. I could watch from afar what he did with my mom's money at that point, although Allen would be more limited without access to donation checks from mom. How he'd gotten her to address them to him was beyond me.

"He'll be demoted, but I prefer to keep an eye on him."

"Ah, keep your enemies close?"

He grinned, and my heart skipped a beat. No man had a right to be that sexy and fierce at once. I was pretty sure most straight women would have sighed along with me.

He topped off my drink. *How did that get so low?* I glanced at his. Good, he'd finished his. I snagged another piece of cheese and one of the summer sausages in hopes of helping with the alcohol consumption. We needed bread.

I couldn't squelch my curiosity about Trey and figured that once our little scheme was over, I might not have another chance to be alone with him. "What do you do in your spare time? There's no video game console, and if there are books, I haven't seen the room with them in it yet." While beautifully decorated, it lacked the personal touches like a book left on the table… it was too neat.

"I'm not here to do more than sleep that often. This is where I crash when I'm too tired to drive home after a long shift, which is all I've had since residency. All that personal stuff is at my family home."

"So this is a crash pad." I frowned. It made me realize I hadn't been brought into his personal space or life, not really. My only glimpse into him would be from what he chose to share.

"I usually spend my free time with my family or doing things Marco tasks me with. Tell me more about you. What do you like to do other than play video games with your best friend?"

"As odd as this is, I get a thrill from hacking into accounts or ending up in digital locations I shouldn't be in." He wasn't on the legal side of the law all the time, either, so I admitted it freely. "If my mother had had her way, I never would have gone to MIT and would have been attending social events and fundraisers like she does. But that's not my thing. Instead, I've embraced the college-dropout role and do what makes me happy. Aside from the occasional coding and video game marathon—okay, often with that one—I love to read, watch movies, and hang by the pool when it's hot outside."

"The computer stuff is what Nico likes to do too. He's got an insane talent for it."

Too bad that's not the brother that makes my pulse go wild. Nico was hot, as was Marco, but I didn't have the same reaction to them. I hadn't met them officially, but I'd seen them before at the Coffee Stop.

Trey set his empty glass on the table then turned toward me, the flames from the fireplace battling the shadows in the room and casting a warm glow on his olive-toned skin, highlighting the sharp angle of his strong jaw. I sipped at my drink, hyper-aware of his leg touching mine.

"It's getting late, and I've got a conference call early tomorrow morning." Trey stood and gathered everything but the drink I'd curled my hands around. I forced myself to get up and followed him into the kitchen. "What I can't figure out"—he set everything down, took the glass from me, then stepped close and brushed a stray curl behind my ear, and I shivered in the wake of his touch—"is why Sofia never introduced us."

Me too. "As I said, I've only met her for lunch or coffee outside of shopping. But we had met before."

"I remember that night well. And I'm sorry for the way I left things."

I shrugged, doing my best to make it seem as if his rejection hadn't cut me to the bone that night. "I understand. Sofia shared a little with me."

He towered over me, and I had to tilt my head back because of how close he was standing. My gaze darted to his unwavering stare. Then he threaded his fingers with my hand. His dilated pupils crowded the warm brown of his irises. Excruciatingly slowly, Trey bent toward me, and I held my breath in expectation of what he was about to do.

In the gentlest of caresses, his lips brushed over mine. Pings of electricity followed in the wake of the kiss, and I leaned into him, my other hand resting on his solid chest, wanting more. Locked together in the tender moment, a jolt of desire hit me like a bolt of lightning. Heat pooled low in my stomach, and he urged me closer so that my body was flush against his. On a gasp, my lips parted, he deepened the kiss, and the world blurred in a breathtaking rush. A burst of need sizzled through me at the connection I felt at his touch, and I gave myself over to it, never wanting it to stop.

Trey

Kissing Hailey hit me with an intensity I couldn't deny. The kiss was meant to be a peck goodnight, a gentle brush over her lips, and nothing more. But everything changed in the moment we touched. My head buzzed with desire—I had to have more of her.

The warmth of her skin urged me closer, and we pressed our bodies together. I devoured Hailey's soft lips. A sexy moan slipped from the back of her throat, acting as an aphrodisiac, fueling the powerful desire that'd sparked from the first touch of the woman I'd found myself inexplicably attracted to from the start.

The hold I had on my control thinned as we kissed, and I knew I would have to stop or I would urge her to take things to the bedroom. It was too soon for both of us. When I drew back, my body fought me. The sensation of holding her in my arms was something I'd never experienced before. There was no explanation beyond it feeling right. She fit. I reluctantly slowed the tempo of our frantic kiss to what it had been when we'd first touched, a tender caress. Her grip tightened on mine, and I slid my other hand from the back of her neck, easing away so there was an inch of space between our bodies. I rested my forehead against hers for a moment then slowly untangled us.

Her lashes fluttered open, and her vibrant green eyes met mine in an unfocused daze that called to me, attacking my resistance. I stepped farther away, breaking the addictive contact.

"What was that?" Hailey swayed unsteadily.

I lightly grasped her hip to steady her, secretly pleased she'd been as affected as I was. "That was worth exploring"—my voice was low and raspy, riddled with want—"but not tonight." I guided her in the direction of the bedrooms. "Get some rest. We'll talk more in the morning after my conference call."

I stood there another couple of seconds after she'd disappeared into her bedroom, the shock at what had happened and how I felt keeping me rooted to the spot. I'd mourned Teresa's loss as though she had been the one, but that kiss had just blown that theory to hell. It shook me to the core.

I gripped the back of one of the living room chairs as the

sound of Teresa's light and bubbly laugh filled my mind, and my eyes drifted shut. She'd allowed me to forget who I was, in a way. Her carefree smile and easy vibe let me slip into the skin of a regular guy.

I could never hide the omnipresent threat of violence, given my family. The way I would react if there was trouble and the deep, instinctive drive to protect those I loved that would surpass anything else. She'd known that about me. It would have been impossible not to. But she'd acted like I was another college guy and would insist we go out on dates to the movies, to get ice cream, to walk on the goddamned beach without guards. She wanted to be normal because that was what she was. And for the short time I was with her, I pretended.

Hailey wasn't innocent like Teresa was. Not fully. She bent the law to her whim, something my family did all the time. I couldn't deny the way I felt with Hailey, but I wasn't ready to let the memory of my time with Teresa go just yet. I ran a weary hand over my face and pushed away from the chair. I needed sleep and to examine what I could potentially have with Hailey with a clear head.

As I passed her closed door on the way to my room, I paused, my hand halfway to her doorknob before I caught my subconscious intent and pulled back. Even though I knew I shouldn't, I stood there for a moment, listening. No sound came from beyond her door. My room wasn't far, and I forced myself to go inside and shut the door behind me before I peeled off my clothes and dropped them on my way to the bathroom. After brushing my teeth, I face-planted onto the mattress, shut my eyes, and fell into a deep sleep.

CHAPTER NINE

HAILEY

My face heated as my fingers fluttered to swollen lips that still tingled from his touch. Realization set in that I'd kissed the guy I'd been secretly crushing on for over a year, and my heart stuttered.

When he'd eased back after the kiss then put added space between us, it could have devastated me, but his huge pupils told me he was just as attracted to me, even if the timing wasn't the greatest.

With the bedroom door shut behind me, I leaned against it, pondering what the heck I was going to do. I'd already decided to stay. With someone as powerful as Trey La Rosa taking on my quest, it just made sense. Something inside me clicked, and for the first time in a long time, I felt like I was where I was supposed to be. I pushed off the door and headed to the bathroom to get ready for bed. It was going to be a long night filled with dreams of that kiss.

Hours later, I awoke to sunlight spilling into my borrowed bedroom. I shoved off the blue-gray blanket that matched the accent wall behind the headboard. It was day two of my grand plan to ransom the money from Allen. I felt the second hand on the clock like a ticking time bomb for several reasons. The priority was to find and redistribute the cash to where it should have gone in the first place, but another issue taunted me—the finite remainder of my stay with Trey.

I pushed the worry aside for later and slid my legs over the side of the mattress until they rested on the pretty rug that reflected the colors in the room. It covered a portion of the light-colored wood floor and was warm beneath my feet.

After a quick shower, I used the new toothbrush I'd found in the bathroom the night before. I got dressed in the only clothes I had—gross. But at least I'd washed my panties in the sink before I'd gone to sleep. Fortunately, they were clean and dry by morning.

Back in the bedroom, I bent to retrieve my sweatshirt from where I'd dropped it. After threading my arms through the sleeves, I pulled it over my head and adjusted it until the soft material hung in place. I'd done the best I could with my hair, which wasn't saying much. I wasn't willing to let it bother me.

When I went into the main living space, it was to find Trey already seated at the island with a serving of eggs in front of him. He turned when I neared. His smile was blinding, and my stomach fluttered in response.

"Morning." Then he dragged forward another plate that had been blocked from my sight. "I made some for you too."

"Thank you." I sat next to him at the island, hyperaware of how close he was. If I moved my arm even a little, I would be touching his. We ate in companionable silence, which I was grateful for, as my thoughts were all over the place—the memory of the kiss we'd shared the night before hung in the space between us.

Trey eyed my shirt. "We need to get you some clothes."

I flashed him a smile. "I'm ready."

"Give me a second."

He went in the direction of his room to change, and I realized I didn't have shoes, just the fuzzy socks I'd put on when I was at Justin's.

He came back in jeans, a Henley, and a gun in a holster strapped to his chest. He grabbed a jacket that hid the weapon then looked at me. I pointed to my feet. "Slight problem."

He scratched the side of his angular jaw. There was a dark coating of scruff, and I loved it. The whole situation was strange, but especially the two of us working together to knock Allen down a peg or two. I had an urge to get ahold of Sofia to see what she thought, but we weren't close enough to text—we only ran into each other now and again. I'd never pushed to do anything more. I had Justin… he was enough of a friend to fill most of the voids in my life.

"I don't have anything here that would fit your feet. If you don't mind, I'll carry you into the store. We'll get shoes there too."

I shrugged, trying not to look too excited by the fact that he would be holding me against his body again. "Okay. It's not like it's the first time. I should be used to it by now."

He laughed, and I hoped he didn't mean he would carry me in a fireman's hold. That would have been embarrassing. After he handed me a long coat, we took the elevator to the underground parking garage that housed what looked like his cars and probably his guards'. True to his word, he lifted me effortlessly into his arms, and I wrapped mine around his neck.

Once in his Maserati, we left the parking garage and headed toward Michigan Avenue. I assumed he was taking me to the boutique I knew his sister liked to frequent. I did, too, so that worked for me. I relaxed in the leather seat as the scenery of the lake on one side and buildings on the other flew by.

We pulled up in front of the shop, and a black SUV containing two guards parked behind us. True to his word, Trey went around the car, opened my door, then lifted me from the seat and into his arms. He kicked the door shut then headed to the boutique, not setting me down until we were inside.

A few browsing women stopped what they were doing to stare at Trey openly. They didn't even spare me a glance, which I was happy about, but at the same time, I was annoyed that they were sending him sensual looks. He wasn't mine, though, and I didn't have any right to get possessive. As soon as he set me on my feet, his phone rang. He grimaced then motioned that he'd be in the corner, taking the call.

A tall woman dressed in Chanel and her hair in a chic bob approached, and I grinned at her. "Hey, Celia," I said to the store manager and head saleswoman. "I had a little shoe and purse mishap."

Her sculpted brows rose, and an amused smile curved her burgundy lips. "I see that. We have a few new pairs of cute boots in, or were you thinking flats?"

"The boots, a pair of flats, and for a coat..." I scanned the store and spotted a midlength one that I loved immediately. "The hooded sheepskin."

"I'll have them at the counter while you shop."

Smooth. But she was right. I needed clothes.

"Except for the boots? You want those now?"

"Yes. Thanks." I headed to some sweaters and fitted pants that I knew would be buttery soft and hold their shape beautifully. I didn't have a ton of patience for shopping, so I grabbed what I thought I would need. I took a quick trip to the dressing room and changed clothes, happy to be out of my dirty ones. Back on the sales floor, Celia dropped the boots by my feet, and I slipped them on, happy not to be walking around in socks.

When I was done making my selections, I took everything to the counter, ignoring the other women sneaking looks at Trey.

"All set?" Celia asked.

Good thing he took me here instead of somewhere else. At least I had a card on file. "Yes. Just charge everything to my account."

Celia looked uncomfortable as she kept her gaze firmly locked on mine. "I can't do that."

"What? Why not?" I had my trust. The credit card was in my name and in no way linked to my mom or Allen.

"Dr. La Rosa is taking care of everything."

That was when I noticed the black credit card in her hand. I nodded, and she visibly relaxed. It wasn't her fight, and I did not need to make things difficult for her. As she got everything rung up, I went to where Trey stood, still in the same corner, snapping something at whoever was on the other end. When he saw me standing in front of him, arms crossed, he grinned.

He said goodbye to the person, pocketed his phone, then took my elbow without a word. Celia had everything in garment bags. After Trey took his card and thanked her, he motioned for one of the guards to take everything. The other was at the exit.

The bell chimed overhead as we left the shop. I glanced at Trey as his gaze swept the area. Then his fingers tightened, and he yanked me close. A loud pop sounded, and I flinched, my phone flying out of my hand and landing with a sickening crack on the pavement. I half turned, and my eyes went wide. The bullet had hit the window behind us. The glass hadn't shattered —it must have been bulletproof—but there was a mark. And it was situated on my side.

All I could do was stare in wide-eyed horror as Trey pulled his gun out and fired several shots.

He barked something at his guards. I stayed focused on him, trying hard not to let panic consume me. He crowded me, using his body to shield mine as he maneuvered me to the car. I clung to him as he fired more shots. Trey yanked open the passenger door then pushed me into the car. More gunshots went off as I fumbled with my seat belt with fingers that refused to work. It took two tries to secure it.

Two seconds later, he rounded the car then was in the driver's side, and we peeled out of the parking spot and onto the road, my heart thudding loudly in my ears. I had a death grip on my seat and the dash as we swerved through cars. His face was like granite, emphasizing his angular jaw and intense eyes. I wanted to ask what the hell had happened, but my heart was pounding too hard, and my stomach churned. I was afraid if I opened my mouth, I would embarrass myself by throwing up all over the place.

In the side mirror, I saw his guards following in the black SUV. It didn't look like anyone else was behind them, but I didn't know for sure—that had been a first for me. Tears pricked the backs of my eyes, making them burn. I refused to let them fall.

The shot had come close to me. I had been the target. There was only one person who would wish me ill, and I wasn't thinking of my old boyfriend from college. *My God, how could he?* It was the only thing that made sense. It couldn't have been anyone else. He was a class-A douche, but having me killed was beyond the pale. My mouth was dry, and my hands shook. *Allen tried to kill me. What threat am I to him that would warrant my death? And what could he possibly gain?*

CHAPTER TEN

TREY

I pushed the Maserati's pedal to the floor, weaving in and out of cars. We were on the highway for a short time, and the exit to my family's home loomed ahead. Before we'd left the boutique, I'd told Sam, one of my guards, to call my brothers and alert them to the situation and where to meet me. I had no doubt he'd also called the rest of the bosses. And if they came, the wives would too. Hailey's stricken expression and death grip on the car hadn't escaped my notice.

"Where are we going?"

"My family's home." I checked the mirror every few seconds to make sure we weren't followed by anyone other than my security detail. As we closed in on the house, some of my rage dissipated enough that I could talk to Hailey without sounding like a complete asshole. "Are you okay?" I knew she wasn't hurt. The shot had gone wide.

"Yeah." Her voice trembled. "I can't believe Allen hired someone else to kill me."

I clenched the steering wheel harder. The turn for the street that would lead to my family home was just up ahead. I hung a sharp right. "He may have involved me with the hopes that something would go wrong, but the terms were never to kill you. And there was no exchange of money, in case you're wondering. Not that I ever would have done anything like that." I didn't need to, and my loyalty was to the family. Always. Odd jobs as a hitman weren't my forte. "But I'm not entirely sure the hit was from Allen."

"Then who?" Her hand shook as she tucked her wavy hair behind her ear.

"That's what I intend to find out." I pulled into the driveway, got out, then went around to her side and opened her door. We had men patrolling the perimeter of the house, but I wasn't ruling out a threat and scanned the grounds while I took her hand and led her into the house. I breathed a sigh of relief only when the door shut behind us.

Sofia appeared from the second-floor landing. As she descended the stairs, recognition flitted across her features. "Hailey!" She grinned. "What are you doing here"—her sharpened gaze read my expression for what it was—"with my brother?"

"Hey, Sofia." Hailey glanced at me. "Sort of a long story."

Laughter trailed behind Sofia as she came toward us. "Those are always the best kind." She winked at me then grabbed Hailey's hand, breaking our connection as she dragged her toward the kitchen.

I watched them retreat, giving Hailey a reassuring smile when she glanced over her shoulder once before they were out of sight.

With my sister taking care of Hailey, I headed toward the office, where Marco had texted that he would be. When my phone pinged, I checked the incoming text to see that it was from Mom. Her message managed to ease a small part of my worry. Katherine was doing well, completely taken with Vincenzo and challenging him from the get-go. The bone marrow transplant was scheduled to happen in four days. I shot off a reply then pocketed my phone.

On my way down the hall, I placed a call to the hospital and asked for Sandy, the head nurse who handled the scheduling if an emergency came up. She needed to know that I wouldn't be in for at least a week. When she answered, I told her as much. She didn't protest or cite rules that we both knew I wouldn't follow. I appreciated that about her. There was absolutely nothing Allen or the board could do about it.

The door was open, and I walked into Marco's spacious office with its large mahogany desk, several chairs fanned around its front, and a couch and coffee table at the opposite end of the room. Bookshelves lined the wall behind Marco, and sunlight streamed through the three windows across from the entrance. I faced him, dropped my fists to the top of his workspace, and leaned forward. "We were shot at today."

A half smile curved my brother's face. "You say that like it's an unusual occurrence in our lives."

"Hilarious." I pushed off the desk then sat in one of the chairs opposite him. "I was with Hailey. The shot went wide. Which means it's either someone who can't aim for shit or Guido is here." Guido, the underboss for Leo Amato, was from New York. He and his henchman had had a beef with Summer the month before and had come to Chicago to try to take her. But Luc, the new Brambilla Mafia boss, had claimed her. We'd taken up the fight with him.

"There were no eyes on the shooter?"

"No. I fired back then got Hailey in the car, and we headed here."

"Let's back that up a little. Why do you still have Hailey with you? I thought you were going to go in, get her, then drop her off at her daddy's."

I opened my mouth to answer but stopped when Enzo walked in, followed by Stefano and Max. All the bosses were present but Luc, who was in Italy, on his honeymoon with Summer. Nico wasn't there yet, either, and I needed him to help with the cameras.

"My wife kicked me out of the kitchen." Enzo cracked me on the back of my head. My fingers itched to grab my gun, but I shot him a glare instead. "Want to tell us who the woman is she's talking to?"

Marco filled them in with what he knew about Allen, Hailey's stepfather, asking for my help, how I'd found her with Nico's assistance, and that for some reason, I hadn't returned her. When everyone was up to speed, I told them the rest. As I was relaying what had happened half an hour before in front of the boutique, Nico entered the room, which was good because I didn't want to explain a second time.

Nico took the seat next to me. "You kept her?"

Marco laughed. I glared at him. He had to have known that much because the guards that had gone with me in response to his orders would have reported it to him. It seemed that he didn't clue in Nico, though, and Sofia hadn't spilled the details I'd shared with her, which I was sort of glad about. It wasn't anyone else's business.

Frustration welled in my chest. "What is with all of you? Focus. I need to know who took a shot at us. I'm not even sure who the target was."

Marco grinned, and his green eyes lightened with mirth. "This is so unlike you. Isn't it, Nico?"

I glared at my oldest brother as my hand went to my gun, and the guys burst out laughing. At least Nico had the sense to take Marco's laptop, spin it around, and type something. He was the one I needed the most help from.

"You're all assholes." There was no bite behind my words. I was the one that didn't usually take things too seriously, aside from when I was in doctor mode. I knew they were enjoying the scene, and I also understood the source of the problem—Hailey.

It happened to all of us—first was Max with Lil. Enzo had always been a fool for my sister. Stefano would do anything for Emiliana. And then Marco. When he found out Elena was alive, nothing could have stopped him from going after her. Nico and I were the last. And Tony, but something told me his cards were different. I could have been wrong, though.

And the more time I spent with Hailey, I realized just how off I had been about the depth of my feelings for Teresa. Hailey was well on her way to owning my heart.

Hailey

As soon as Sofia saw, she'd dragged me away from her brother and into the living room. I'd shed my new coat, draped it over the back of the burgundy couch, then kicked off my new boots and curled my legs under myself. Sofia perched on the love seat across from me.

"Love the boots," she said. "Now, what the heck are you doing here with my brother?"

Before I could answer, a door slammed off in the distance and hijacked Sofia's attention. Not even five seconds later, Elena, Lil, and Emiliana swarmed the room. The only one I knew was Sofia, but the other wives were equally as stunning, and I fidgeted in their palpable confidence. Power radiated throughout the room. I had no doubt it rivaled their husbands'. Trey wasn't a boss, but he shared the same fierceness.

I'd done my homework—or stalking, as Justin would have said. A small smile curved my mouth because he would have been right there with me, obsessing over how hot they were, even though I had eyes only for Trey. Something about him drew me—even the photos of him posted online were captivating. A connection, even if imagined. That was what I'd thought then, prior to the night of the fundraiser. Now, after reconnecting with him, I knew I was right.

Emiliana took the seat next to Sofia. Elena claimed a tan club chair, and Lil sat on the other end of the couch where I was.

Sofia made introductions. "Okay, we're all here." She grinned. "Now, spill. What're you doing with my brother?"

"He crashed my pseudo abduction in my best friend's basement."

"Come again?" Mirth colored Emiliana's words.

Sofia smirked, and Emiliana shoved her. "You knew?"

"Seriously, Sof." El frowned. "We missed out on an opportunity to harass him. That's just not cool."

Lil laughed, and Sofia waved them off. "I know all that, yes, but not why she's here at the house. That's…" She met Lil's gaze across from her.

"Yeah," Lil said. "It's sort of a big deal."

"Anyway"—Sofia brushed aside Emiliana and Elena's earlier comments with a wave of her hand—"continue, Hailey."

I gave them a brief rundown of what Justin and I had done, the video, Allen involving Trey to find me, and how Trey had flipped the kidnapping to his favor.

"The guys are having a meeting," Elena said. "Does it have to do with you?"

"I'm not sure. Someone fired a shot at us when we were leaving a store."

Lil's light gaze swept over me. "Neither of you were hurt?"

I shook my head. "No. The shot was way off, from what he said."

"Huh. Well, whatever. We'll hear about that when they're done." Sofia dismissed the topic. "What I want to know is what's going on between you and my brother because I've never seen him like this."

Emiliana's eyebrows furrowed. "Not even with Teresa?"

Sofia pursed her dark-red-stained lips. "Nope."

"Interesting," Lil said. "Are you and Trey dating?"

"I hope so." Sofia squealed.

I couldn't help but laugh. "No, we're not dating." I had a feeling she knew about my infatuation for him, though. "I don't think he'd be interested in me." The humiliating rejection from the first time we met reared its ugly head. And his interest in me now? I was there, so that made things convenient. I couldn't read too much into anything. I wasn't even in the same league as the guy, regardless of how much Justin swore I was.

"Think about it." El brushed her unusual caramel-highlighted warm-brown hair over her shoulder. "If he wanted to screw with Allen, that's one thing. And I get it because I've met the man. Can't say I like him."

"Nope. Not even a little," Sofia chimed in.

"He could have dumped you at the hospital and wiped his hands of the mess," El reasoned. "But he didn't, which is typical of our guys." She winked at Lil, who burst out laughing.

"There was some seriously hot chemistry between you two when you came into the house," Sofia said through her chuckles.

"There was not." I tossed a pillow at Sofia, who batted it away, completely unperturbed. I breathed a sigh of relief. I was lured into a heady sense of belonging from how they were joking with me and including me in the conversation. But these women were badasses and not to mess with.

"Stop overthinking, Hailey." Sofia rolled her eyes. "I've known you for a while, and don't think I didn't notice the way you would drool over any tidbit of information about Trey." She leaned forward and stage-whispered, "Don't tell my other brothers, but he's my favorite."

El snorted. "I might tell Marco that."

Sofia picked up the pillow and launched it at El faster than I could take my next breath. I waited for violence to erupt. I mean, I'd heard the stories about the gunfights and more that they were involved in. When all El did was snicker, I let the tension drain from between my shoulder blades.

Lil cleared her throat, and I turned in her direction. "In all seriousness, we need to help this situation along."

A grin curved Sofia's mouth in a manner that could only have been described as sinister. "Couldn't agree more."

"Wait a second." I needed to stop whatever train they were riding. "There's nothing to help along here. I'm staying at Trey's place until we can get the ransom from Allen. I'm sure he'll kick me out as soon as the money is delivered."

I wasn't sure I liked the speculative gleam in Sofia's eyes. I'd never been lucky in love and didn't want to read more into anything than was there. Trey and I had shared a kiss that probably meant way more to me than it did him. Besides, Trey falling for me could never work—he'd already shown me that I wasn't anything special.

CHAPTER ELEVEN

TREY

I ignored everyone but Nico. "Check the security camera at the boutique." I restlessly tapped my foot. I thought I heard a smothered laugh from Enzo and sent him a death glare.

Enzo held up his hands. "Done. Swear it. But you're both fine, and if the bullet was way off target, it's hardly a threat. An enemy to be concerned about would not have missed."

"I understand that, but—"

"I've got something," Nico interrupted then swiveled the laptop so we could all see the screen, split into two images. "This angle here"—he pointed to the left—"is from the shop. We can only see a blurry image and not enough of his face to get a good visual. But we can from the restaurant across the street."

I grinned. "Guido Amato." After our run-in with the Amato underboss, I would have recognized his beady eyes and receding chin anywhere.

Max smacked me on the shoulder, and I shared a dark grin with him. "This should be fun."

The desk chair squeaked as Marco leaned back. "He's a glutton for punishment. I'm not even sure he's worth the effort of grabbing him."

"Luc would think otherwise—"

"It's a war we'll have to engage in if we kill him," Marco interrupted Max. "Guido's a tool. And before we do anything definitive, we should alert the New York families."

It was my fault that Guido was after me in particular. I'd told Luc where to aim to render Guido's hands incapable of accurately shooting a gun. At least until he had several surgeries, and even then, he might not recover the full range of his fine motor skills. It was a fitting punishment and one we'd delivered. It also saved his father from having to mete out his own reprimand. "Wonder if the Amato boss knows his son is here?"

"Doubtful," Stefano said. "I'll reach out to Leo Amato and, as a courtesy, to Dante Verretti."

We had an open line of communication and a level of respect with the Verretti crime family. The other two families that ruled there, Amato and Tucci, were irrelevant. They were so low on the Italian-American Mafia syndicate's radar that they were laughable, something that disturbed the two families enough to do foolish things, like taking a potshot at Hailey and me. I wasn't sure I could let go that her life had been threatened. But I would wait to see what Stefano discovered after speaking with two of the bosses in New York.

"What are you doing about Hailey?" Stefano leaned against the wall, crossing his arms over his chest.

He was our capo, and I had to answer a direct question whether I wanted to or not. "For now, I'm keeping her." I clenched my teeth. The thought of her leaving my place didn't sit right. "There's something strange going on between Allen and Hailey, and I'm not sure it's only on her end. It's better she stays with me until I figure it out."

"At least we know that Guido isn't in Italy and after Luc and Summer." Enzo moved to the other side of the office.

"True." It didn't add up that someone wanted Hailey dead. Me or anyone else in the Mafia, sure. We had plenty of enemies

—which we took care of. But I knew enough to listen to my gut. Even with the confirmation that it had been Guido taking shots at me, I couldn't shake the sense that she was in danger.

Stefano hit the contact number for the Verretti boss then put the call on speaker, and we fell silent, waiting for it to connect. On the third ring, a deep baritone crackled through the line in greeting, to which Stefano responded, "Dante, we have a problem." He held his phone in front of him. "You're on speaker."

"Who else is there?" Dante's voice growled through the office.

Stefano listed off our names. "Guido is in Chicago, taking potshots at my family."

Dante grunted. "When you sent him back the first time, I thought Leo would take care of him. What are you going to do?"

"I'd prefer to end him here."

"It would start a war," Dante said.

"One you would join in?" Stefano's voice held a warning.

"No. I don't want to jeopardize the truce between my family and the Five Families. I vote to start a war. Eliminating the Amatos is one less problem for me to deal with."

"Sounds fun." Enzo smirked.

"Is Leo a problem?" Stefano asked.

"Leo is ambitious, but he's smarter than his son," Dante said.

"I'm placing a courtesy call to Leo. If he wants us to deliver his son, I'll allow it. This once. But if Guido steps foot in Chicago again, all bets are off."

"Let me know the outcome," Dante said.

After disconnecting, Stefano called Leo, the boss of the Amato family. "Your son is in my city. You have two choices: plan his funeral or pick him up from the airport when I tell you and make sure he never sets foot here again." He paused, listening. "I'll be in touch with the details." After another brief pause, he hung up. "He chose option two."

I stood, not happy with the decision. Given the silence in the room, no one else was, either. The meeting was over. I opened the door and walked out. They could keep talking if they wanted, but I was done. My only thought was to get Hailey back to my place.

"Hey," Nico called after me. "I met Hailey on my way in here."

I knew that tone in my brother's voice. I turned and bared my teeth at him. "She's with me. Back the hell off." Hailey had more in common with Nico, at least in a computer-geek kind of way. But she was mine, or she would be. I didn't want Nico messing up what was developing between us.

"It's like that, huh?" A slow grin spread across his face.

"You're the last man standing, Nic," Marco said with a chuckle.

Enzo pushed off the windowsill and headed my way. I didn't like the glint in his eyes. "Let's go meet this woman."

Great.

Max smacked me on the shoulder as he moved past. I followed with Stefano and Marco trailing behind. I had a distinct feeling that we were embarking on one of the war games we used to play out back. If teams were forming in a Hailey inquisition, I needed to get her out of there. Once I caught up with Enzo, I shoved him into the wall, getting ahead and zeroing in on my brother, who'd just cleared the kitchen and pivoted toward the family room where the girls congregated.

"Nico," I growled in warning as he sat on the couch between Hailey and Lil then went to put his arm around Hailey. The fucker. One year separated us, and I wasn't having it. Long strides ate up the distance between us, and I curled my fingers around his shirt and pulled him up despite the twenty-odd pounds of muscle he had on me. I wasn't going to point that out. "Back off."

A slow smile curved Hailey's lip. "So this is your brother? The banker?"

Nico shoved my hands off him before turning to face her. "And the better-looking one."

I cracked him in the back of the head. Hailey raised an eyebrow, and a spike of something went through me, throwing me off-balance. I couldn't have been jealous. We'd only known each other for a short while. Marco went to stand by Elena. His hand slipped beneath her hair, resting on the curve of her neck.

"You don't have to live with this guy." Nico aimed his thumb in my direction.

"Really?" Hailey pursed her lips, appearing to contemplate the move. "What are you offering me, protection? I've got that with your brother."

Stefano held out his hand to Emiliana. She stood and leaned against his side. He wrapped an arm around her waist, watching Nico try to move in on Hailey with amusement. I was going to kill my brother.

Sofia snickered behind me, and I shot a glare her way. "Not helping."

"I've got your back." Enzo lifted Sofia in his arms then took her seat, settling her on his lap. He winked then started to make out with my sister.

"What the hell?" I would need to wash my eyes out.

"Get your tongue out of my sister's throat," Marco roared while the girls laughed. I could see the humor and almost thanked Enzo for what he just did, but it was gross. With the distraction, I swooped up Hailey's coat from where she'd dropped it on the back of the couch, grabbed her hand, and pulled her to her feet. Then I maneuvered through everyone while my brothers argued with Sofia, who was furious that they thought they had any right to dictate what she did with her husband.

I sighed then yelled over my shoulder that we were leaving. I owed Enzo, and I didn't like it. Once we were by the front door, I helped her into her coat before opening the door. Fat snowflakes fell in lazy swirls before adding to the blanket of white that covered everything in our path.

Hailey shivered, and I pulled her close. "Not a fan of the snow?"

"I like it when I'm inside and warm."

I couldn't fault her logic there. It was still early, before lunch. As I opened the passenger door for her, an idea popped into my head—a particularly appealing one after the bullshit with my brother. He was trying to get a rise out of me, and I was annoyed that it had worked. He'd done the same thing with Teresa at *The Coffee Stop*, but it hadn't bothered me.

I pressed the start button on the Maserati, and the engine roared to life. We traveled down the long driveway, past the gates, then onto the road heading toward the highway. Only, we weren't heading home. I had other plans in mind.

CHAPTER TWELVE

HAILEY

The scenery flew by in a blur of cars and white tufts of snow. I should've been nervous because of the road conditions and the sports car, but I wasn't. Trey's confidence obliterated any need for worry. As the miles ticked along, I couldn't help the warmth in my stomach over the way he had reacted to his brother's teasing. Trey hadn't liked it, and that made me pause. There was no denying that I had feelings for him, and I wondered whether he had them for me.

When we merged onto another highway, I pulled myself from my thoughts, not recognizing the new route. "Where are we going?"

"To the airport."

"Why?" With the ransom deadline the next day, I wasn't sure I liked the change of plans. At least my clothes from the boutique were in the car. He took his eyes from the road, and I sucked in a breath at the visible emotion.

"Why not? We have the time, and I'm not due back at the hospital for a week. Let's go to the Caribbean, soak up some sun, and walk on the beach."

I laughed, feeling carefree and happy for the first time in… I couldn't even remember when. "Well, when you put it like that."

Trey's grin was wicked, and I prepared myself for a wild ride. He floored it, and we got to the airport in half the time. No commercial flight for us. He'd called ahead, and his family's jet was ready and waiting for us. Everything moved quickly from that point. We boarded into the lap of luxury with captain's chairs that fully reclined, a gourmet lunch, and even a bedroom in the back, which we did not use.

Less than four hours later, we were off the jet and in the sweltering humidity of Grand Cayman. A car whisked us to a sprawling beachfront mansion complete with an infinity-edge pool and hot tub.

Out of the car, I lifted my hair off my neck as we walked to the front door, trying to stop the thick strands from adding to the overwhelming heat. "Please tell me the house has air conditioning."

Trey entered a code into the security panel then pushed open the door. A waft of chilled air beckoned, and I readily followed it inside. "Is this your place?" It was beautifully decorated—white walls with pops of colors in varying shades of blue and gray. It was elegant but still had a beachy vibe.

"It's family owned." Trey walked toward the back of the house, and I followed.

Mostly floor-to-ceiling windows and a giant slider that led to the back of the house came into view as I entered the kitchen and living room. Water views were showcased from every window, and I fell in love. If I could have lived there, I would happily have done so.

"I thought we'd take advantage of the house being empty while we can," he said before opening a door off the living room, which had a shiplap accent wall. "Sofia's bedroom is at the end of the hall and on the right. You can borrow clothes and a bathing suit. She won't mind."

I wandered into a spacious bedroom and got hung up on the view again. The closet caught my eye—another room in itself but fitting of Sofia—and I hurried to find a bathing suit to wear to take advantage of the beautiful weather while I could. I picked out a black bikini, found a hair tie, and did the best I could with my hair, which was expanding into a mass of curls. It took some effort, but I managed to gather it into a messy bun.

My pulse jackhammered as I looked around the spacious bedroom. *What am I doing?* I liked him. A lot. But my track record with men was dismal at best. My insecurities bombarded me, as did the worst dating experiences from my past.

My best friend wasn't the only one who had terrible luck when it came to love. At least Justin wasn't awkward and destined for catastrophe. Case in point was my ex, Jacob Martin, the reason I'd left MIT. Jacob had been the star pitcher for the baseball team, highly sought after with his Ken-doll all-American good looks. I didn't normally go for those kinds of guys. Not since the nightmare of my fourth grade first love who'd decided to show the notes I'd passed him to the entire grade.

My sister had been the opposite. Guys panted after her. She was the "it" girl, always had been, at home and at school. That didn't matter to me because she was also my best friend. Kasey always had my back—my stupid crush in fourth grade found that out the hard way when she publicly blackballed him from kickball for what happened to me. Then she told everyone the notes were his, and he'd pawned them off as mine. My sister was awesome like that.

Then she'd died. Dad too.

Lonely, desperate for physical contact, and mourning the loss of half my family, I'd tried again at the end of middle school to another disaster of epic proportions—Steven Riley, a member of the popular clique. When he'd asked me out, I was thrilled, and rightly so. Every girl in school was in love with him and apparently knew him on an intimate level.

He was my first. I'd thought it was love. We'd gone on a double date. His brother had driven to the movies, and we'd stayed behind while they went in to get their tickets and popcorn. Steven dumped me right after we'd had awkward sex. I mean *right after*—I hadn't even gotten out of his brother's rusted hunter-green Bronco. Once I'd managed to yank my clothes back on and scrambled from the back seat, I caught Steven and Melissa Johnson, the head cheerleader, meeting up on the theater's steps.

I was the weird girl—a mathlete and computer geek. Apparently, he didn't want to be seen with me or my flat chest—his words, not mine. In high school, my boobs came in, and I told him to suck it when he noticed. *Asshat.*

Wary, and for good reason, I'd avoided anything serious in high school. It wasn't only that. I missed my sister and my dad, and the fact that my mom was emotionally absent didn't help things. Justin did. If it hadn't been for him, I didn't know what would have become of me, especially after Jacob. He'd demolished what remained of my self-confidence.

Sex with Jacob was mediocre and not like what the movies or books portrayed. The relationship wasn't all bad, though. He was okay to spend time with, when he wasn't going on about baseball or telling me to watch him play. God, that was like an all-day event—*and outside*. I wasn't having it.

As the weeks bled into months, he guilted me into doing other things for him because I wasn't a supportive girlfriend. He had plenty of support from all the other girls sucking up to him since he was rumored to be headed to whatever it was baseball players went when they were professional. *NFL? No, that's football.* I had no clue and zero interest in sports.

With my crappy luck in love, it was clear the problem was with me. I was unlovable. That had to be, because I was intelligent—I had proof of that. But I clearly lacked judgment. I picked up on signals from people easily on a daily basis in every arena unless when they pertained to my love life. I should have suspected something was off when Carly, the blond knockout who hung around the team like a deranged superfan, kept showing up wherever Jacob was.

But we were solid, or so I'd thought.

All those favors—grocery shopping, buying him the new cleats he couldn't afford or the whatever thingy he needed for the sport—hadn't bothered me. What did was the night he freaked out because his coach had talked to him about his grades. He needed to get an A to pass a class. That was where I came in. I helped, even though my instincts were screaming at me to run far and fast. I hadn't listened. Instead, I'd logged into the school's mainframe and changed not just one of his grades but several.

I was a sucker.

He'd used it against me later, when I caught him macking on the blond bombshell. Things got ugly when I told him to go to hell and started packing up my stuff. He'd slammed the door shut and barred me from leaving. He said if I did, he would tell the school what I'd done, and I would get kicked out. Not him. He and the bimbo would testify that I'd done it without his consent and that he was with her when it happened.

I was so screwed.

In the middle of the night, while the fucktard was sleeping, I'd taken my things and left, not just his apartment but the school too. Justin knew what had happened. No one else. My mom bought my drifter sob story about how I couldn't figure out what to major in and it was all a waste of time, anyway. She'd thought that in the beginning, so it wasn't hard to convince her.

After that nightmare, I'd sworn off men. I could fantasize about them, though. Relationships conjured in my head were perfectly okay. It just so happened that my number-one dream guy—key word "dream"—was Sofia's brother, Trey, the consummate bad boy who had a good side who was a doctor, at least from what was apparent from my pseudofantasy relationship. But then he'd walked away, and I'd felt so rejected, even though I'd learned he was still mourning his ex. I shouldn't have held it against him.

Even so, trusting a potential, real-life boyfriend was hard. And sometimes, I was a bit defensive. But who could blame me after a shittastic past like mine?

I should have been worried about getting mixed up with Trey.

But this time, I'd been smart. I'd looked at what he could gain from me at every angle. I had time to think about it after all. There was nothing I had that he needed. Allen? The spot on the board? I wasn't naïve. He didn't need Allen to make that happen.

My trust fund? Not a chance. My family may have been one-percenters, but our net worth was chump change compared to the money he had. And the only other thing I could think of was my hacking skills. But even there, his brother Nico and whoever else they could easily employ filled that nonexistent void.

There was nothing I had that Trey could use me for. Nothing. With that in the forefront of my mind, I wanted to try one last time. If I was wrong, and the relationship failed, I was done. I wouldn't hitch my ride to another guy for the rest of my life. It was my last attempt at love. I only hoped I didn't sabotage it with my abandonment issues and defensiveness.

My mind was made up, and I shoved aside the insecurities brought on by the bad choices in my past.

I took one last look in the mirror, noticing the determined gleam in my eyes before leaving the room and making a beeline for the back doors.

CHAPTER THIRTEEN

HAILEY

Trey was already outside and in the pool. As I slid the door open, a wave of heat blasted me. Two brightly colored towels were thrown over loungers at one end. Sunscreen sat on the small table between them. Even though it was late afternoon, the rays were still powerful, and I could feel their effects on my skin. While Trey swam laps, I slathered on a good coating then sprawled across one of the chairs to let it soak in and do its job.

The sound of the waves combined with Trey's rhythmic laps lulled me into a light sleep as the sun warmed my skin. When drops of water landed on my stomach and a shadow blocked the sun, I blinked my eyes open to Trey standing over me. My gaze crawled hungrily over his disheveled dark hair to follow the trail of several droplets as they ran from his hair, over his wide shoulders, then down washboard abs.

I pushed up onto my elbows, my mouth suddenly dry. Words failed me. All I could think of was tracing the path of a drop of water that rolled lazily down his chest.

"Let's go for a walk on the beach." Trey extended his hand.

I shook myself from the mesmerizing hold he had over me,

swung my legs over the side of the lounge chair, then put my hand in his, letting him help me up and welcoming the warm breeze coming off the Caribbean Sea.

Even with the sun sinking in the sky, it was a beautiful, cloudless day. Trey clasped my hand in his as we padded down the private boardwalk that led to the long stretch of beach. This was heaven. All I needed was a drink in hand, and I would never want to leave. My soul felt lighter, and I left my problems in Chicago, where they would wait for our return. I desperately needed the reprieve.

"How often do you come here?" I'd never been to the Cayman Islands, and so far, it was ranking in my top-ten must-visit places.

"Not enough." His voice held a wistful quality. "Nico can get away and come here with the excuse of work. There's a financial hub on the island. But I have a lot of memories from when I was a kid, and our dad bought the place for our family as a getaway. Mom loves it, as it's very different than Italy."

"It's lovely here." My toes pushed off the soft white sand. Just shy of turquoise water lapped at the shore. I wished we had time to stay longer than one night.

"The people are amazing. They're very family oriented. One time, my mom walked to town with the four of us. Sofia was a baby. It was crazy hot, and by the time we had picked up a few things, most of us were tired and hungry. Mom decided to take a cab back, not knowing the driver was on his lunch break."

I laughed. "So you all had to walk anyway? I feel for your mom."

"You would think, but no. The driver insisted on taking us because of 'the kids.' He also refused to accept payment."

"Did he know who your mom was?"

Trey stepped over a broken conch shell. "I don't think it would have mattered. The native people are just that way.

Family is everything to them. They watch out for one another's kids, whether they're from here or visiting."

We turned around to head back, walking in companionable silence, saying hello to the few people we passed. I got the feeling that his family welcomed the residents onto their property with open arms. No one showed fear or wariness around Trey. It was also the one place I'd noticed that he didn't have his gun strapped to him twenty-four seven.

I cast another longing glance at the stunning water. He tugged on my hand, angling us so that we were facing the sea. Then we waded in. Warm water lapped at my legs the farther in we went. When it was up to my shoulders, we stopped, buoyant in the salt water.

Trey's hands found my waist, and an electric current from his touch shimmered over my skin. Then there was the way he was looking at me. My heart skipped a beat, and I swayed toward him, helpless against the magnetic pull. His gaze dropped to my lips then slowly returned to my eyes. My hands settled on his wide shoulders, and the muscles bunched beneath my fingertips as he inched me closer.

"That kiss we shared last night."

The memory of his lips on mine seduced me, and I shivered from the sensual onslaught. I caught my lower lip between my teeth then released it, waiting for him to continue.

"I can't stop thinking about it." He lifted a hand from my waist then traced my bottom lip with the pad of his thumb, trailing droplets of salty water in its wake. "There's something between us, and I want to explore it."

I tilted my head, confused. *Does he want something purely physical with me? Because I'm on board with that, but I need clarity to do a better job of guarding my heart if that's the case.* "You want to explore what?"

"A relationship." His thumb rested over the pulse fluttering at the base of my neck. "Are you interested?"

I slid my hands up his neck to tangle in the thick, silky strands of his dark hair. Our chests pressed together, and I gasped at the contact, a breathy "yes" following before his lips slanted over mine.

Heat built between us as he deepened the kiss. The water lapping around our entwined bodies faded from my awareness, as did the diminishing sunlight. The way he touched me went beyond anything I'd ever experienced. It was soul searing and life altering.

I could have continued to devour him, but he changed the intensity of the kiss until his touch was tender rather than earth shattering. When he pulled back, all I could do was cling to him. The only thing that appeased me when he broke the kiss was the way his heart thundered against my chest and the raw hunger swirling in his dark eyes.

"We should get out of the water and go back to the house."

I worried my lip. Things were spinning out of control. I needed a moment to catch my breath.

He grinned as if reading my mind. "We'll shower and change then go get something to eat."

"Yeah, okay." I put my hand in his, and we made our way through the water then up the boardwalk until we reached the pool area, where we'd left our towels.

I borrowed one of Sofia's sundresses, and we had dinner on the terrace of a beachside restaurant, complete with twinkle lights overhead. I glanced at the menu and decided to have their fish-of-the-day special, paired with white wine because a piña colada would not have gone well with that meal. Later... I would definitely order my favorite beachside beverage. After our wine was delivered, I couldn't refrain from asking Trey what it was like growing up.

"I can't imagine what it was like as a kid, growing up in one of the Five Families."

Trey grinned. "There was always danger, but my family

handled it in a manner that didn't cause us undue stress. Unless someone got shot." He shrugged. "We were close. Marco and Nico were more similar, so Sofia and I tended to hang together if there were conflicts between the four of us. The worst was when Sofia wasn't included. It was rare, but it happened."

I leaned forward. "I can't imagine she dealt with that well." She struck me as such a force, confident and determined but still fun and adventurous. People were drawn to her charisma, which had instantly ensnared me.

"No." Mirth danced in Trey's warm brown eyes. "One time, and I honestly don't remember what Marco had done, but Sofia snuck into his room when he was sleeping and put makeup on him. He had a habit of wandering downstairs half asleep for breakfast, so he didn't realize he was wearing blue eyeshadow, hot-pink lipstick, and these two streaks of bright-red blush on his cheekbones."

"That's not so bad."

"It wouldn't have been, if we hadn't taken pictures and used it as blackmail for years."

"Sofia was the biggest troublemaker?"

Trey snorted. "Not really. We were pretty young when this happened, but Sof and I had done something to Nico. Neither of us know what it was—we'd just borrowed it, but I guess we erased a program he was working on. Anyway, he retaliated by cutting five inches off Sof's hair. He did the same to me, but he buzzed it."

My jaw dropped, and outrage on Sofia's behalf blasted through me. "I would have shaved all my sister's hair if she did that to me. Then added permanent marker to her face in the form of a mustache."

"Yeah, well. My parents put a stop to it because things had gone too far. Nico was grounded, but so were we. It was a pretty awful two weeks. Mom made us do everything together, rotating through things each of us liked. If anyone complained, a day was added and filled with the thing we complained about. It was brutal. Sof was into this fashion video game... I wasn't. Pure hell, let me tell you."

"Oh, poor you." I snickered. "But I bet she was devastated about her hair."

"She was. Sof rarely cries. If someone outside of our family makes her, they pretty much fear for their lives. It's probably only happened once. That night, she stayed in my room and bawled for hours."

"I don't think I would react well to that either. But at least Sofia probably looked beautiful, shorter hair or not."

Trey furrowed his brows. "Hailey, have you not looked into a mirror?"

"I try not to." I rolled my eyes, uncomfortable with the focus shifted to me.

"You're gorgeous. How do you not know that?"

"Thank you." Heat climbed into my cheeks, and I took a hasty sip of my wine. "Was it always Sofia against the three of you?"

"No. A lot of times, Sof and I were a team. She always had my back, and if I needed to talk to someone, nine times out of ten, I would go to her instead of our brothers."

I liked their dynamic, but it made me miss Kasey even more. "Did you have many friends outside your family?" I honestly didn't know how the Mafia worked.

"Of course. But it was easier with the others—Enzo and the rest of the guys. We were all around the same age and spent so much time together. Friendships with people not in the Mafia could be dangerous—to them."

Sensing he was done with that line of talk—it probably reminded him of those he had lost, like Teresa—I shared more of my experience at MIT, including the messy breakup, and he seemed genuinely interested in my experiences.

After dinner, we ordered to-go cocktails and strolled along

the beach. The night was magical. I felt at ease with Trey and capable of talking about anything, and I got the impression that he did too. His phone rang, and I waved away his apology. He was a doctor and in the Mafia, and even though he was off, I could imagine there would always be important calls he'd have to take. Oddly enough, I was okay with it.

He wrapped his arm around me and pulled me close as he laughed at whatever the other person said. I had been more content in those six hours than I had been since my sister died. I never wanted the day to end.

———

Trey

I hung up with Vincenzo, chuckling. The water lapped at the shore in a soothing repetition, and I looped my arm around Hailey's waist, resuming our walk along the beach. Stars twinkled overhead, growing brighter the farther we got from the seaside restaurant.

"What was that about?" She matched my pace, tilting her head to meet my gaze.

"I sent a friend of the family, Katherine Armond, to stay with Vincenzo, Lil's grandfather, in Italy so she can receive specialized medical treatment. He was calling to update me on the demands Katherine has made."

"I take it she's a handful."

"And then some." I laughed again, imagining the uproar she was creating in his life. He needed some shaking up. "She's amazing. He's annoyed because she's barged into his room on more than one occasion and demanded that they go for a drive."

"Shouldn't he be doing those things, anyway, if she's his guest?"

"Yes and no. He's Vincenzo Brambilla, Italian royalty." I

grinned at her. "She threw out his cigars."

"Oh."

"He doesn't know what to do. I wish I could've seen her in action. My mom's been texting me updates me here and there. From what she's said, there's something brewing between them."

"You mean they're interested in each other?"

"Yeah, but he's fighting it every step of the way."

Hailey kicked at the water as it rushed over her foot. "Sounds like that would egg her on even more."

"I think he's met his match. From what I understand, his wife was a gentle, quiet woman. She loved him fiercely but never opposed him. And Katherine—"

"Doesn't have a complacent bone in her body?"

"Exactly." Memories of one afternoon, in particular, sprung to mind. "This one time, Sofia and I went with Mom to Katherine's small makeup studio. I can't remember what we did that made mom yell at us, but Katherine would hit us with a rubber band gun when we weren't looking. There were others in there, and it took a while to figure out who was doing it. Katherine's poker face is legendary."

"Oh wow, I think I love her."

"She's amazing. I could have sent her to another one of our houses and hired a few nurses to care for her, but I had a feeling she would hit it off with Vincenzo, at least eventually." He grinned. "I thought about visiting her after the ransom is over, but if Vincenzo is calling and complaining, I don't want to give him an excuse. He needs to get out of his own way and realize he's interested in her. She's just not what he's used to, and he's been alone for a long time."

Our fingers entwined as the shrill ring from my phone shattered the peacefulness around us. I answered without looking at the caller ID. Allen's voice grated through the speaker: "I know you have her."

CHAPTER FOURTEEN

HAILEY

The glow from his phone highlighted the hard glint that had entered Trey's eyes, and I froze. He either hated whoever was on the other end of the line or had just gotten bad news. I shivered—not from the cold but in anticipation of his reaction.

"Justin snitched."

What? My head snapped back. I couldn't have heard him correctly.

"Interesting."

It had to have been Allen on the other end of the line. A mix of anger and fear warred inside me, and I pressed my lips tightly together to maintain my silence.

Trey paused to listen to whatever Allen had to say. At least I knew who he was talking to. I was also confident that Allen wouldn't go to the police with what Justin had allegedly told him. Allen hadn't so far. It would only shed light onto his crooked business dealings.

"I have plenty of ways to keep Hailey here." Allen must have replied during the silence. "The terms stand." Trey disconnected the call with a slow, menacing smile. "Seems your friend ratted you out, and right before the ransom is due."

I stood at a precipice of uncertainty, my heels inches from the waves breaking on the edge of the shore. Justin would never have sold me out. We'd been friends for years, and he'd always been there for me, no matter what mess I'd found myself in. "It couldn't have been him."

Trey grasped my arms, anchoring me to the present. I could barely make out his expression with the silvery glow of the moon and stars overhead our only source of light. Our perfect evening slipped from the tips of my fingers. We wouldn't be able to stay the night, and I felt the loss of what I would have experienced in his embrace vanish, all from one phone call that had changed everything—again.

Allen was bad juju. There was no way around it. He was a problem.

"He won't do anything." Trey's deep voice sent a shiver of awareness down my spine as he pulled me close. "I promise you'll be safe."

Cocooned in his embrace, my concern faded, and I let him carry the burden, if only for a short while. But that wasn't my way. I was used to taking charge. I had been responsible for myself for most of my life.

I stepped back. "Something is very wrong if Justin went to Allen. I can't imagine why he wouldn't have called me if he had doubts about my safety with you. That's the only reason why he would call Allen."

"Do you have your phone on you?"

Goose bumps danced over my skin in a rush of adrenaline-fueled alarm. "I don't. It flew out of my hand when we were shot at. It's lying on the sidewalk in front of the boutique. I heard the crack when it hit the ground, and we were moving fast. I forgot about it in the heat of the moment."

"You trust him?" The skepticism in Trey's voice was loud and clear.

"One hundred percent." He had no reason to trust Justin, but I'd known him forever. We'd been through more than two friends should in a lifetime: the loss of my sister and dad, Mom's remarriage, a horrible breakup in college, a few failed relationships of his, and my sense of failure after dropping out of MIT. I had no doubt that he had my best interest at heart. Justin was my ride or die.

"He must have tried calling you and panicked."

"I'm sure that's what happened. I need to get ahold of him." I held out my hand. Trey pulled his phone from his pocket, unlocked it, then passed it to me. Good thing I had Justin's number memorized. With the phone pressed to my ear, I paced along the shore. I could feel Trey's eyes on me the entire time. *Come on, pick up.*

When the call rolled into voicemail, I used the time the best I could. "Justin. I lost the phone. It was a total accident. I'm fine. I swear it. This is Trey's number. Allen called. *He knows.* I don't know how much, but he knows I'm with Trey. *Please call me.* I need to find out what you told him. I'm not mad. Promise."

After disconnecting, I handed back Trey's phone. My stomach was in knots. I knew Justin, and once he heard my message and realized he'd screwed up, he would beat himself up about it. The guy took things way too hard. I knew we would find a way to salvage the situation so that the kids would still get the money and Allen wouldn't have access to it. I had faith in my new accomplice.

But that meant we had to leave and do damage control. "We need to go back home."

"It would be wise," Trey murmured. He curled his hand around mine and pulled me in the direction of the restaurant, where we'd left the car. "We'll have to change our tactic with Allen. I'll continue to pressure him for the ransom with the angle that you'll be harmed. In the meantime, we'll follow the money trail."

"I need a computer." I should have been working on that all along. I let myself get distracted by having Allen withdraw the cash, but Trey was right. We needed to take down wherever he was stowing his nest egg of Mom's money.

"I'll have Nico drop one off. It completely slipped my mind to ask him before." He pulled out his phone and shot off a text before putting it away again.

I briefly squeezed his hand. "I'm sorry. I wish we could have stayed longer, but I'm so glad we got to spend at least some time here."

He released my hand then wrapped his arm around my waist, drawing me close. I snuggled against him. Lights twinkled ahead, and the faint sound of conversations danced above the rhythmic rolling water. He drew me toward the boardwalk that led to the restaurant, and we left the firmly packed sand near the shore, the dry granules shifting beneath our feet. We reached the boardwalk, and my heart pinched at the thought of leaving it all behind. I wanted to spend a month there with Trey. The island was so peaceful and laid-back, not at all like the defensive and hectic vibe in Chicago.

We walked along the weathered planks then trekked the short distance to one of the small observation decks where we'd left our shoes. Trey bent before me, and I rested my hands on his shoulders as he brushed the sand from my feet then slipped on my sandals. He got his shoes on, and we headed toward where he'd parked the car.

Trey opened my door and then rounded the vehicle to his side and got in. The engine purred to life, and we meandered through the streets with the windows down, letting in the balmy salt-laden air until we arrived at the house. It wasn't far, and we could have walked if it hadn't been dark. I wanted to drag my feet and return via the beach rather than the car, prolonging our exit off the island. *If only.*

The driveway was ahead on the right, and Trey turned in, the garage door raising as we neared. He pulled in and shut the engine off, and we got out. My heart was heavy as we walked inside to cool air blanketing us and causing me to shiver.

With the flick of a switch, Trey turned on the lights, and the mudroom was illuminated, as was the hall that led to the open-concept floor. My gaze was drawn to the outdoor living area, where the water in the infinity-edge pool softly glowed as if inviting us outside. I slipped my sandals off. The tiles were cool beneath my feet as I padded toward Sofia's room. "I'll only be a minute."

"Take your time."

I paused, my hand on the door as Trey passed to go into his room. The white button-down he wore stretched tightly across his wide shoulders, tapering down to his narrow waist. Beneath the thin material, his muscles bunched and flexed, and I longed to run my hands over them.

Once he was in his room, I entered Sofia's. We hadn't brought anything with us but the clothes on our backs. After changing, I went to stand by the sliding glass doors that led to the pool. Strong arms slipped around my waist, and I leaned against his chest. He rested his chin on my head.

I was worried about my best friend and what Allen might do to him. Even though he couldn't turn either of us in to the police, part of me thought he had it in him to hurt Justin—maybe not physically, but somehow. He had no ties to Justin like the one he had to me, and Allen's coldness extended to his business dealings. Too often, when he was conducting a meeting in the office at home, I'd heard him make threats.

He had something on Justin, and that was what I worried about most.

"Everything will be okay." Trey's arms tightened ever so

slightly. "Justin will call back, and we'll find where Allen is hiding the money."

Justin took priority over screwing over Allen. "I hope he calls soon."

"How important is it to recover the ransom?" Trey turned me in his arms so that we faced one another. "I'm asking because I'll donate to the children's fund tonight if that's your biggest concern."

Touched, I reached up and curled my hand around the back of his neck, urging him to lower his head. When he did, I brushed my lips across his in a tender kiss before drawing back. His magnetic pull made me want to keep kissing him, but I needed to get the rest of my thoughts out first.

"I want the money to go where it belongs, so yes, that's very important to me. But whether it's today or tomorrow doesn't matter. I understand that you're asking because it's very likely Allen won't hand over the cash now that he knows you have me. Why, I'm not sure, unless Justin told him we faked the abduction and that you aren't holding me against my will." He cupped the side of my face and brushed the pad of his thumb along my cheek.

"There was something in Allen's voice that didn't sit right with me. He's either on to us, or he just doesn't care one way or the other what the outcome will be. It's unlikely he'll deliver on the ransom tomorrow."

"Do you think he'll do anything to Justin?" My fingers tightened around the fabric of Trey's shirt. I had my instincts, but I trusted his more in dangerous situations. We came from very different backgrounds, and of the two of us, he had a vast amount of experience over me.

"What could he do? Going to the police will only spotlight him, and that's the last thing he wants. Justin doesn't work for the hospital, and I doubt Allen cares enough to cash in any favors to get him fired."

I rested my cheek on his chest and breathed in his scent. "You're right. He isn't that dedicated to anything. The most important thing to Allen is himself."

He kissed the top of my head. "Let's head out. The pilot will be at the jet by the time we get there if we leave now."

On the way out, he turned off the lights before leading me to the front door, where a car waited to take us to the airport. He locked up as the driver got out of the car and held the door open to the back seat for us. I climbed in then scooted over to leave room for Trey. When the car door shut behind him, the driver got in, and we pulled away from the best surprise I'd had in a very long time.

All the sunshine, swimming, drinks, and stress over Justin must have caught up with me because one minute, we were pulling away from his family's gorgeous home, and in the next, Trey nudged me awake. "We're at the airport."

I shivered from the effects of his deep voice. He helped me out of the car, and I walked beside him in a daze. We boarded the jet, choosing to sit on the couch along the side of the luxury cabin. I managed to buckle my seat belt and tuck myself into his side, and he wound an arm around my shoulders before my eyes drifted shut.

My eyelids briefly fluttered open when Trey carried me off the jet and again when we arrived home. Back in the room I'd been occupying in his place, I was vaguely aware of him slipping my shoes off and pulling the blanket over me. He bent and brushed a kiss against my lips. My fingers trailed over the fabric of his shirt. "Did he call back?" I had to know.

"Not yet." He pulled the blanket up and covered me, chasing the chill of the room away.

I wanted to pull him into bed beside me and snuggle into his arms, but my mind had other plans as I slipped back into a restful sleep.

But then I huddled under the covers as a dream invaded my

peace. In the dreamscape, dark clouds rolled overhead. I was outside with Trey, near the boutique. Lightning flashed, charging the air. Thunder rumbled, rattling the panes of the storefront windows, and I clung to Trey's hand as we raced down the sidewalk, unsuccessfully dodging fat drops of rain. The world was sepia, warning us of danger, of bad omens.

The fine hairs on my arms stood on end as goose bumps rose. A blinding bolt of lightning struck the ground several feet in front of us, followed by a sonic boom worthy of a landmine—the explosive expansion of air launched us from our feet. Trey's hand tore from mine. I screamed his name. Then my body dropped to the cement, pain radiating from the impact and leaving me stunned for more seconds than I was comfortable.

Frantic, I rolled to my side, the rough concrete scraping my palms as I pushed myself to my knees. Amid jarring, angry claps, the sky strobed overhead. I peered through the unnaturally dark greenish-yellow atmosphere as familiar loud pops pierced my heart with numbing fear.

I crawled forward and spotted Trey lying unmoving a few feet from where I'd landed. I screamed his name to no avail. My trembling fingers gripped his lifeless hand, the cold from his skin seeping into mine, reaching deep into my bones. His eyes were staring sightlessly at the raging sky. Red bloomed in several spots across his chest, and the water spread and muted the color but not the meaning.

It was my fault. Death was meant for me. But again, it'd missed its mark and taken another I loved.

CHAPTER FIFTEEN

HAILEY

I awoke on the wrong side of the bed, the nightmare plaguing me all day. We were back in Chicago and smack in the middle of winter rather than enjoying warm temperatures and strolling the beach at Grand Cayman Island. Lake-effect fog rose in the distance, swirling and wafting inland to dance over the shoreline's frozen waves. The sun was barely up, and an uncontrollable restlessness made me jittery with the need to do something childish like flattening my hands against the pristine slider that led to the balcony, leaving prints.

Justin going to Allen then ghosting me was messing with my attitude. Trey's phone hadn't rung once during the flight with a callback. Not finding Justin and talking him off the ledge he was undoubtedly using as a dramatic stage was making me crazy. Not only that, but I couldn't help but worry about how much he'd told Allen.

If I didn't get out of there and stretch my legs, I wasn't sure what I would do or say, and that was never good. From the direction of the study, I could hear Trey moving around. Whatever call he had to take had ended a few minutes before. The

108

heavenly aroma of coffee lingered in the air from the cup I'd already consumed. One was never enough.

"Morning." His deep voice preceded him, and I turned in his direction.

With my back to the view that had taunted me, I arched an eyebrow. "Is it?" I bet my hair reflected my out-of-control mood. The wavy dark curls had a mind of their own sometimes.

Trey looked as drool-worthy as always, but I focused on how trapped I felt. And while I could have vegged for days on end, it needed to be by choice. Instead, I felt like my decisions had been taken from me—which was my fault, in a way, but I didn't want to acknowledge that. It stemmed from returning to a winter landscape and the aftermath of my nightmare. Trey's heightened sense of security back in the city was another factor. "I'm going crazy. Let's go for a walk on the beach."

"It's freezing out."

I shrugged. "Doesn't matter." *I want to feel in control.* "I need to get out and stretch my legs." I tracked him as he went to the kitchen and got the coffee machine going for the second time that morning. "Besides, it's early. I'm sure all the assassins are still asleep at this hour. And Allen doesn't roll out of bed until nine at the earliest. So our bases are covered."

"Cute." He chuckled. "You think we work on a schedule? No killing until after dinner?"

I shrugged. I had no clue. "It's not my profession. Educate me." His grin was infectious, and my agitation thawed a little.

"If a hit is put on someone, there are rarely time restrictions. You're fair game to the assassin, day or night." He poured his coffee into an insulated to-go cup then got another from the cabinet. A surge of hope shot through me.

"If Allen is looking for me, which is unlikely, it's not going to be at this time of day. And I doubt that Guido guy is a morning person, either. Plus, he's a lousy shot." I gravitated toward the coffee he held out to me. "We can have some guards look out for us too."

"I don't have any arguments."

I grinned, and I curled my hand around the insulated cup. "You want to get out of here too."

"With you, sure."

Warmth spread through me, and I released the coiling tension that had spurred my crabby and sarcastic mood. He paused and slid something over the large island. I glanced down to see a new iPhone in front of me. "You got me a new phone?"

"Yeah, since your last one was lost. It might be easier for Justin to call you back on your line. That could be why he hasn't contacted you yet."

"You're probably right. Thank you."

He winked, and butterflies took flight in my stomach. Ignoring them, I tapped in Justin's number and waited for him to pick up. When he didn't, I left him another voicemail then fired off a text. It was too weird that he wasn't responding.

What I was feeling must have been all over my face because Trey came around and pressed a kiss to my forehead. "I'm sure he'll call soon."

I hope so. We put on warm coats, hats, and gloves then took the elevator to the ground floor and exited to the lakefront side of the building. After a quick word with his security team, Trey stayed close as we made our way to the beach. A bitter wind tore through the open area, stinging my cheeks. It didn't matter. I was happy to be outside, even if I missed the warmth of the Caribbean. But I needed the fresh air after that tormenting nightmare.

"We won't go far," Trey said as he tucked me closer against his side.

It was freezing, and I was almost second-guessing my insistence on going outside, but stretching my legs and feeling a sense of freedom helped. I felt better already. It was hard to walk with his arm around my waist, so I pulled away then looped my arm through his instead. We trekked across the frozen sand at a good pace, and my blood warmed from the struggle to keep up with his long stride. "Do you miss staying at your family's home, since it's so much larger and there are more people around?"

"I see them often, so no, I don't miss it. At least, not with you here. I would go stir-crazy after a day or two if it were just me. Do you miss your home?"

I snorted at the absurdity of the thought. "No. Not even a little." A sharp pang pierced my heart, and the truth followed. "That's not entirely true. I don't miss what it's like living there now, but there are memories I have a hard time walking away from. My sister's ghost walks the halls. I see her laughing at the island, the smell of chocolate chip cookies in the air. Or in the media room, watching a movie. Then there's her room. It's remained untouched since she died. The first year, I would climb into Kasey's bed and sleep with her vanilla-caramel-lotion scent clinging to the sheets and pillow, like she was still in the room with me. Then Mom found me there one day and completely freaked out. I took one of Kasey's candles from the room, and when I'm missing her, I light that instead."

"It had to be hard to leave all those memories. You're truly not happy living there any longer?"

I tilted my head, taking in his larger-than-life presence with the arctic background of the semifrozen lake and dense white clouds overhead. He walked beside me like a force, and the power emanating from him only heated my blood more. "No. I don't want to live there anymore. I should have moved out a long time ago."

A sensual grin curved his lips. "Stay here with me."

I tripped over my own feet, and his arm tightened on mine, steadying me. I must have misheard him. "Are you asking me to move in with you?"

"I am."

I opened my mouth, but nothing came out. "Shock" was an understatement.

"Look. You're here now. Just stay. You can look for a place on your own time, but it's better than living somewhere you don't feel welcome anymore."

Oh... so a temporary situation. That, I could get on board with. It felt more like a friend helping a friend out, aside from the seductive grin that I refused to read into. A shiver racked my body, and Trey promptly turned us around, and we headed back to the townhome.

"Okay. I'll stay here until I figure something else out." Just saying it lifted a huge weight from my shoulders, and I laughed.

"Then it's settled." He tugged me so that I was in front of him.

He pulled me close, his mouth dipping toward mine as his phone rang. Reluctantly, he eased back, withdrew it from his pocket, then looked at the screen just as mine chimed. I vaguely heard Trey answer, but my gaze was riveted on my phone. The text was from Justin and simply said, "I'm sorry."

I tore off my gloves, and my fingers flew over the keys. The longer I typed, the more the cold seeped in and made them stiff and harder for the keyboard to register. After I tapped send, I waited. There weren't any dots indicating Justin was typing. Nothing. Impatient, I hit the button to call him, pressing the phone to my ear as I slid the gloves back on my frozen fingers.

It rang until his voicemail picked up. Shocked, I didn't leave a message and hung up instead. Emotions ping-ponged through me—I was confused, upset, and angry. I didn't understand why he was acting that way. It was like Darrengate all over again—Justin had been dumped by a very hot but pretentious Wall Street guy he'd been dating for six months. He'd fallen into a pit of despair, and it'd taken me practically breaking down his door then forcing him to talk to get him out of his funk.

Did telling Allen send Justin into a tailspin? Intense worry broke through the anger of being ignored. I needed to know he was okay and not curled up in a depressed ball on his bed while reruns of *The Office* or *Supernatural* played on his TV. I could envision the floor strewn with empty pizza boxes and wine cooler bottles.

Trey's growl snapped me out of my thoughts, and my gaze shot to his irate one. I'd forgotten he'd answered a call. *Who is he talking to? Could it be Allen?* The ransom was due that day—not that I was under any illusion that he would follow through, knowing I was with Trey.

My ears strained to make out what was being said. Fortunately, I could hear because both sides of the conversation. Allen screamed that I'd made a mess, and he wasn't going to lift a finger to help get me out of. I wasn't his problem.

"But I am your problem." Trey disconnected the call then shoved his phone into his pocket. He urged me to move with a hand on the small of my back.

I quickened my pace as we went back to his place. Trey's features were granite, and if I hadn't known him, I would have been terrified. I didn't question what was going on or why he was so angry. The fact that Allen didn't care about my well-being was no shock, but it had set Trey off. We passed his security then went through the door on the first floor and straight to the elevator. It wasn't until we reached the top and had piled our coats on the back of the couch that he turned to me.

"Allen isn't going to get away with how he treats you."

I closed the distance between us, my chilly hands clasping his. "And he won't. We're going to find out what he's doing with that money then take it from him. I just need a laptop."

Dark promise swam in his brown eyes. "Nico dropped a laptop off while we were gone. It's in the office."

A thrill raced through me at the prospect of digging deeper into whatever trail Allen had left. "Is Nico searching too?" It would have been fun to work with another hacker, who might have a few tricks I didn't already know about.

"He'll have more time at night. Give me your phone. I'll put his number in there."

I handed it over, and he added Nico to my contacts. "Thanks." My body was buzzing with the need to get on the computer, but in the back of my mind, the issue with Justin kept hammering away like an angry woodpecker. "I need to check on Justin." I tapped the messages app and showed Trey the single apologetic line.

Trey's expression became guarded. "He responded, so you know he's okay. There's no way you can go to him. Allen probably has someone watching."

"What does that matter?" I took a step back, frustration making my voice increase in volume. "Allen won't do anything. He refuses to pay the ransom and has washed his hands of all of it. Why would he care if I was at Justin's?"

"I don't trust him, and I won't take a chance on anything happening to you."

I braced myself for the fight that was brewing. I was coming to know that fierce expression and what it meant, but I was equally as stubborn. "I'm going. He's my best and oldest friend."

"Please, Hailey. I'm asking you to hold off. Keep trying to get Justin to open up over text or call him. I'll have one of my security guys drive by his place and get a visual, so you'll know he's okay. In the meantime, I'm going to pay Allen a little visit at the hospital."

"When you say you're paying him a visit, do you mean to kill him?"

Deep laughter warmed the living room with his vibrancy. "No. I'm not going to kill him. I'm just issuing a warning about not going near you. He needs to know that you're under my protection. We'll deal with what he's done with the money as soon as you and Nico find it."

I launched myself into his embrace. It felt good to have someone looking out of me for a change. As his strong arms held me close, my heart pounded against my chest, and I realized just how much Trey was coming to mean to me. He was no longer a crush but someone I could see myself falling for, and that thought terrified me.

CHAPTER SIXTEEN

TREY

I roared through the streets in my Maserati, intent on surprising Allen at the hospital. I'd left Hailey at the house, parked in front of her new laptop and chatting with Nico as they worked their computer magic. She had been confident that she would have a solid lead on the money by the time I got back. I didn't doubt her for a second.

But that wasn't the only thing that needed to be accomplished. My fingers tightened on the wheel as I pulled into the hospital's parking garage, sliding into one of the spots reserved for doctors.

My head of security, Sam, had staked out Justin's house. He'd returned with a picture taken through a kitchen window of Justin rinsing dishes at the sink. Once Hailey saw that, I felt confident that she would stay home while I went in search of Allen.

The ransom deadline had come and gone without so much as a cent from him. That didn't concern me. Hailey and Nico would figure out where the money was, but I had to ensure he didn't mess with Hailey. Allen was petty and vindictive. I didn't trust that he wouldn't make trouble for her.

Dressed in pants, a white shirt and tie, and a black wool overcoat that hid my shoulder holster and gun, I breezed through the ER. The pungent odor of disinfectant heavy in the air, the bustle of nurses as they went about their duties, and the chime when a patient pressed the call button provoked an urge to work. But it wasn't strong enough to deter me from my preordained course.

Sandy, the head nurse, came out of her office as I took the hallway that led to the elevators. She read my expression and offered a subdued hello as we passed each other. The metal door swooshed open, and I rode to Allen's floor then went straight to his office.

The door was shut. I didn't bother knocking. I slammed it against the back wall, and it closed with a loud thwack behind me.

Allen jumped to his feet, dropping the papers he'd been looking over. Alarm pulled his aristocratic features taut. "What are you doing here? You're not scheduled to work."

He'd been checking up on me. I stalked him around the desk, my emotions barely in check. My fingers curled tight on his neatly pressed light-pink button-down shirt, yanking him close so that our faces were inches apart. "Hailey is under my protection. You're not to reach out to her or even say her name without first consulting me. That applies to all areas of her life, professional and personal. Is that clear?"

Allen's eyes widened, fear flashing in the muted blue depths. "Crystal." He snapped his mouth shut, his throat working. I could tell he had more to say, but wisely—for once—he held his tongue.

"Don't make me have to come after you. You won't like what will happen."

His Adam's apple bobbed, and he jerked a nod.

I released my hold on his shirt, smoothed out the wrinkles, then patted his cheek with a resounding smack that was almost a slap rather than a friendly tap. He dropped to his chair as I backed up, not a word leaving his lips. I held his gaze for a few seconds, taking his measure. I hoped for his sake that I'd gotten through to him.

Done with that little chore, I left his office, making my way swiftly through the halls of the hospital and back to my car before anyone could approach me. The time it took to get my point across had been short, but I would still have to keep an eye on him where Hailey was concerned.

The drive home was uneventful, but as soon as I walked into the living room, Hailey's expression said that she'd discovered something.

⁂

Hailey

"We found the shell corporation," I blurted to Trey before he was barely off the elevator. I got to my feet, grabbed his hand, and pulled him to where I'd been sitting. "See?" I pointed at the screen. "This is the account where Nico and I traced the check."

"That's less than you demanded Allen hand over."

"Right." I pushed a mass of dark curls from my face. "Look here. There were two withdrawals on the account, all for large amounts and all in cash." It made sense because I'd asked for cash in the ransom. "That's where the trail ends. Since the bank is in the Caribbean, Allen could have flown there and back."

"I have something to show you." He took my hand, drew me into the study with him, then logged on to his laptop, opened his email, and clicked on one from the children's foundation, a confirmation of a large donation.

I sucked in a breath, tears misting my eyes at his generosity. I turned and flung my arms around his neck. "I can't believe you did that." It was unreal.

"I told you I would." Trey brushed a strand of hair from my cheek and tucked it behind my ear. "It was important to you, and if I hadn't intervened, you would have gotten the money from Allen."

Raised on my toes, I lifted my face to his, my gaze focused on his lips. He didn't disappoint, bending and slanting his mouth over mine. The shell company, the money... everything fled my mind at the brush of his lips. Hands at my hips, he tugged me flush against his hard body. Dizzy with want, I moaned, lost in how he made me feel so very wanted. I clung to his broad shoulders, my fingers exploring as his muscles shifted beneath my touch.

My entire body buzzed. The tempo of the kiss changed. I didn't want it to end. He slowed the insatiable way he devoured my mouth until he broke the kiss. My fingers went to my swollen lower lip where I could still feel his touch, his desire. It hit me then. I would have slept with him. I wanted to.

So why are we stopping?

Then the sound of his phone registered.

"I'm sorry." Regret lined his face as he pulled the phone from his pocket.

I got it. He was a doctor and in the Mafia, a man in high demand. My body didn't agree with sharing him in any capacity, though. I stepped back, and his jaw flexed. I didn't like the separation, either, but our moment was interrupted. Perhaps it was for the best.

He answered and clipped out a response I didn't bother to pay attention to. Once he hung up, he directed all that intensity at me again, stealing my breath and quickening my heart rate.

"I want you more than anything." Trey's desire-laden voice sent a surge of heat through me as he slipped his phone back into his pocket. "I'd planned to come back and take you out to lunch. I don't want to rush you into anything, and we've only been on one date."

I grinned. Best first date ever. "In the Cayman Islands."

"Do you want to go?" His eyes darkened. "Or we could stay here?"

Straightening my shirt, I put more distance between us as I went for my shoes, fighting my body the entire way. After I convinced him to take me to Justin's, it would be nice to go to lunch. "No, let's go out."

Going out without worrying about Allen would be great. Trey had talked to him, so I didn't have anything to stress about. Not that I would have, anyway.

We grabbed our coats. Trey's hand was on the small of my back as we took the elevator down to his car. He had a few words with the head of his security team, Sam, and then we were off, one of the black SUVs following us with two guards inside. It was my chance. We exited the private underground garage, and I shifted in my seat to take in Trey's chiseled profile. "Can we make a stop before lunch? I wanted to check in on Justin since he's at home." Or he had been when Sam took that picture, anyway. I knew his schedule, and he didn't work that day.

"I'm assuming that you're not going to let it go if we don't stop?" Amused eyes met mine before he returned his attention to the road.

"You're correct." I grinned. I relaxed back in my seat, stretching my legs in front of me. It bothered me that I hadn't talked to my best friend and that he probably blamed himself for messing up our plan to get the money back. But I wasn't mad—he was looking out for me. It had been a mistake on my part not to contact him as soon as I knew I'd lost my phone. Maybe he'd been trying to reach me.

It didn't take long until we turned into Justin's neighborhood and found a parking spot on the street not far from his two-story brick bungalow. I shoved open the car door before Trey could come around, and the bitter cold slapped me in my face. Snow lined the narrow parkway before the sidewalk, and I plodded through it with him at my side. I tucked my hand in his, and we climbed the three cement steps to Justin's, where I bent and rummaged around the base of a flower pot with daisies painted on it. The key was beneath the tiny pebbles lining the saucer of the pot. I unlocked the door then pushed it open with the key in hand. Trey closed it behind us as we stomped the loose snow from our shoes then slipped them from our feet to leave on the shoe mat.

"Justin! It's me," I called. "Justin?" The living room was bare as it always was. He'd never bothered to get furniture for it. Bypassing the basement stairs, I checked the kitchen. There was a bowl and spoon in the sink from breakfast. He had a weakness for sugary cereals. Case in point, a box of Fruit Loops was on the counter.

"Maybe he's still sleeping." I grabbed Trey's hand and pulled him with me upstairs and into Justin's room. The bed was a mess, as usual. He didn't see the point in making it since he would be sleeping in it again at night. The rest of his room was immaculate. That was where the neat freak in him came out. He was never in the kitchen before noon, which we were closing in on, so I was surprised he hadn't cleaned up his dishes and put the cereal away. It took him a while to be civil. He was an absolute bear and unfit for company before he'd had two cups of coffee.

The rest of the place was spotless. I checked his closet and bathroom. Nothing was missing. He'd been here. Maybe he'd run out for something.

We retraced our steps and went to the basement. A lone game controller was on the coffee table in front of the leather couch, but there was no sign of him. I worried my lower lip as we climbed the stairs and let ourselves out. After relocking the door and returning the key to its hiding place, we got in the car and headed to the restaurant.

"He'll be back." Trey squeezed my hand, steering with only one of his. "Are you worried because he hasn't returned your call? You mentioned this wasn't abnormal behavior for him."

"Yeah, he will. And this isn't unusual when he thinks he's screwed up badly. It's his process, and he's done it before." I pulled my hand free and rubbed my palms together, feeling shaken. "I don't know. Something feels off."

"I'll have one of the guards keep an eye on the place and alert us when he's back home."

"Okay. That would be good." Somewhat appeased, I tried to push the worry from my mind so I could enjoy our lunch date. A familiar thrill raced through me at the thought of spending time with Trey. I just wished I could share what was happening in my life with Justin. Trey had kissed me, and I wanted to dish to my best friend.

I messed around with the radio while Trey drove too fast down the highway then off the exit. After a few more turns, he pulled up to a fine dining restaurant named Bramare. I glanced at my dark jeans then back to Trey in his black pants as he rounded the car and opened the door for me. "Am I under-dressed?" I'd heard of the place before, and I was positive that jeans weren't included in the dress code. But when we walked through the entrance, warm air greeted us, as did the hostess.

"Welcome, Dr. La Rosa."

"Gina." Trey offered a closed-lip smile.

"Let me take your coats." Trey helped me with my coat then handed both of ours to her. She then motioned to a coat attendant, who relieved her of our outerwear. "Table for two? Or are you expecting guests?"

"Just the two of us."

"Very well. Please follow me."

His hand settled on my lower back again, sending a jolt of

awareness through me as we followed the hostess to a table situated by a roaring fire. Several plants were strategically placed, offering privacy. I fell in love with the dining establishment immediately.

"The Vitale family owns this restaurant. You can wear whatever you want."

"This is Enzo and Sofia's place?" I thought I had the right couple. Sofia, Trey's sister, had married Enzo.

"Yes. I'm surprised you haven't been here with Sofia."

Me too. "We mainly stayed around the boutique. It was casual the few times we got together. Mostly coffee."

The waiter came, and Trey ordered wine for us. I chose the spaghetti alle vongole, in the mood for clams and pasta. He chose the filetto alla barolo. Of course, I had second thoughts and wanted to taste the filet mignon with wine sauce and wild mushrooms.

I took a sip of my wine, savored the spicy flavor, then leaned back in my comfortable chair. "What are you thinking, now that you've had some time off from the hospital?"

He set his glass down and grinned. "It's refreshing. For the most part, I enjoy working there. But the demands of my family are difficult to balance with the hectic and long shifts at the hospital."

After meeting more of his family, I could understand wanting to be there for them. "And you need to be more available?"

"With Marco as boss of our family, yes. There's more pressure."

"Not something you're unfamiliar with." The demands of med school, residency, and working in the ER were intense.

Trey fell silent as the waiter placed our meals before us. My traitorous stomach growled at the heavenly smell of the food. The dishes were a work of art, and I almost felt bad messing it up by twirling some pasta onto my fork.

"It's nothing new, but my loyalty lies with the family." After cutting a piece of filet, he popped it in his mouth.

I studied his features as we chewed. I wanted to know more about him. There was a half-inch scar on his forehead, slightly off-center. "Where did you get that scar?"

"The one on my head?"

I nodded, twirling more of the pasta with a bite of clam.

He chuckled. "Emiliana threw a book at me when we were young, and I refused to let my mom take care of it because I wanted her to see what she'd done. It was stupid, but at the time, I thought it was important."

"What did you do to make her that mad?" I had trouble thinking of the gorgeous woman I'd met throwing anything. She'd seemed so controlled, even if my instincts were screaming to tread carefully around the Mafia women.

He shook his head. "I can't remember what it was about anymore. Emiliana's got an even worse hairline trigger than my sister. I know Nico was involved. He instigated something that I inevitably picked up. Obviously, we were teasing them about something. Anyway, I took the brunt of her anger. Nico took off when she threw the book. Traitor."

"I can picture your brother doing that."

Trey finished chewing another bite. "You saw the joking side of him the other day. He's pretty serious most of the time. He's responsible for the finances of the Five Families. It's a lot. There are times he needs to let off some steam, but it's all in good fun. He's got a huge heart, and he used to have a monstrous crush on Emiliana."

"Isn't she married?"

Trey snorted. "To the capo. And Stefano is very possessive of her."

"Aren't all the guys with their wives?" They made an impression on me. The love they had for one another was tangible, and I ached to have what the Mafia women had.

Trey regaled me with stories of his wild childhood for the rest of our meal. Even with the danger they lived with day in and day out, their closeness and loyalty were apparent. They managed to live each day to the fullest—at least that was what I got from how he talked. The pain of the last handful of years weighed heavily on my heart. I'd wasted a lot of time letting life kick me around. The loss of my dad and sister then the rejection I'd felt on a cellular level from my mom had both hit me hard. The messy breakup at MIT and how I'd chosen to leave, blaming the decision on not knowing what I wanted to do or major in while there instead of facing my problems with my ex, also haunted. It was easier to run, and I'd been doing it for far too long now.

"Do you want to order dessert?"

My hand settled over my stomach, and I groaned. "No. I'm stuffed. It was amazing."

No bill appeared, and Trey stood, offering his hand to help me up. I wanted to ask about paying, but since the restaurant was Mafia owned, maybe he didn't have to. He went to loop my hand in the crook of his arm, but something must have caught his eye. A commotion sounded near the front of the restaurant. Trey pulled me behind him, his hand tight on my arm.

"Stay here, Hailey," he ordered as shouting cut through the muffled conversation of the other patrons. Someone screamed, and Trey jolted forward.

I couldn't see what was happening with his body blocking my sight. Dishes shattered. With Trey farther away, I caught sight of his bodyguards. They all converged on a man.

"I'm going to take what you value most!" the man bellowed.

There was a thump and a grunt, then a gunshot went off. I jumped, my fear for Trey gripping me in a choke hold. *Where did the shot go? Was Trey hit?*

My heart jackhammered against my ribs, threatening to break them. I rushed forward as Trey's fist slammed into the man's face. He crumpled to the ground, and I kicked the gun that had dropped from the stranger's hand away.

Trey turned to me, fury pulling his features taut as he scanned me for what I assumed was a bullet hole. "I'm fine." I flung myself into his arms, uncaring of the scene I was making. His arm wrapped around me like a steel band, and he buried his face in the crook of my neck.

"Christ, Hailey. I could have lost you."

CHAPTER SEVENTEEN

TREY

Hailey's arms dropped back to her sides. I vaguely registered the screams or clink of silverware hitting plates as people rushed to leave. My guards had Guido Amato flung over a shoulder and were heading out. Silence hung in the restaurant as patrons openly stared. It happened so quickly that I knew not all of them had seen Guido's gun. The ones that did were pale, and some even fled toward the front. What a fucking disaster.

The hostess and staff would deal with the diners. They were well versed in how to handle those types of situations. I took Hailey's hand in mine and led her to the exit. Our coats were passed to us, and after helping her, I guided us outside and into the waiting car.

"Are you—"

"Wait until we're inside." I could barely form the words. The red haze hadn't dissipated from my vision. She didn't even appear frightened. The incident shook me more than I'd thought it would. Once we were seated in the car and pulling into traffic, the nightmare of what could have happened exploded to the surface. "This is a bad idea. You shouldn't be with me."

"What are you talking about?" Hailey swiveled in her seat so that her green eyes bored into the side of my face.

"After I deal with Guido, I'm going to take you back to your place." From my peripheral vision, I tracked how she crossed her arms over her chest and the fierceness of her expression. I knew I was in for an argument, but my decision was for the best.

"Whatever's going on in your head needs to stop. I'm not scared. You and the guards were on him before anything could have happened."

"You should be scared!" I roared. Fear for her life was making me crazy. "Have I told you about Teresa?" I took a turn too quickly, the tires squealing in protest.

"No." She tilted her head, her voice no less sure.

"She was my girlfriend. An innocent. She was a barista at the goddamned coffee shop and went to college."

Hailey pursed her lips but remained silent.

"I never should have dated her. She was sweet and kind and not from my world. It was an escape for me. I realize that now. My selfishness came at the cost of her life." I pulled into the driveway of my family's home then slammed on the brakes and threw the car into park in front of the door. After untangling myself from the seat belt and shoving my way out of the car, I went around to her side. She'd opened her door, and I shielded her as I ushered her inside. There weren't any threats. My guards' SUV came to a stop behind us before they roughly extracted Guido from the back. They'd gagged him, so he wasn't spewing stupidity. A hood prevented him from seeing where he was as they brought him into the house.

I didn't need to tell them where to take him. I pulled Hailey through the entryway and into the living room. We remained silent as the guards passed us and headed for the basement.

Once the door was shut and I was confident they couldn't hear us, I turned her to face me. "You could have died."

Her palm rested flat over my heart, and she took a small step forward, her green eyes softening. "But I didn't. I'm fine." A familiar spark of stubbornness showed in the narrowing of her gaze. "And we both know I'm not innocent."

"You are." I couldn't shake the haze of fear and anger as I backed her up to the wall. "If you stay with me, you'll end up dying by a bullet meant for me—*just like she did*," I said through clenched teeth. I couldn't get the image out of my head of Teresa lying in the street in a pool of blood. I had to let Hailey go. If I didn't, she would suffer the same fate as Teresa. And if that happened, I didn't think I would survive.

Doors slammed, interrupting our private moment. Voices filtered through the house. The guys were coming, and I could also hear their wives. I released my hold on Hailey's arms and took a step back. Her gaze stayed locked on me as I put more distance between us. I didn't like the high tilt of her chin or how she pressed her lips together. Whenever my sister did that, we knew there was no stopping her from getting what she wanted and that she would make our lives hell until she got her way. I'd seen flashes of stubbornness from Hailey, but a full-on war like what Sofia rolled out was a concern, especially since my sister had just walked into the room.

Sof's head tilted, and I pointed a finger at her. "Stay out of it." But that was a stupid move. It was like waving a red flag in front of a bull. I needed to get control of my temper or leave the room before I made things worse for myself.

I stole another look at Hailey. Her narrowed, glittering gaze followed me as I moved past Sofia to meet the guys. I didn't need to check that my sister had caught the exchange and would undoubtedly lend her unwanted advice. Emiliana, Lil, and El were right behind her, and I grunted in lieu of a greeting as I exited the room.

Stefano said nothing, just opened the basement door and disappeared down the stairwell. Marco and Nico followed then Max. I could tell they were pissed that Guido was still a problem. I was too. Enzo grinned, slapping me on the shoulder. "Stefano called Dante. He's on his way." Dark intent flashed across his features. "Let's go have some fun."

I could get on board with that. Dante being there was a long time coming, and I looked forward to meeting the Verretti boss.

Enzo and I maneuvered down the stairs then through the large open space in the basement with its oversized flat-screen TV, leather sectional, fireplace, and pool table. There were other things down there we used to play for hours on end when we were growing up, like air hockey, foosball, and a dartboard. Weaving through the furniture, we went to the back wall where there was an obscured door leading to a soundproofed room. After pushing the door open, Enzo and I spilled into the space with the other guys.

Guido's hood had been removed but not the gag. His back was to the door, so he couldn't see behind it when it was opened. I closed the distance between us and ripped the duct tape from his mouth. He yelped from the layer of skin I removed then fixed hate-filled eyes on me.

"You're lucky you're alive," Guido ranted. "You, Luc, and that bitch, Summer, ruined everything." He whipped his head back then spat. It missed his target. Instead, it landed on his shoe, lacking the power to hit me. A thin line of saliva trailed from his lower lip and down his chin, but he didn't seem to notice. "This isn't over. After I kill you and them, I'll find Mia. Things will be as they should."

My brows furrowed. "Mia Tucci? What do you want from her?" She was a Mafia princess belonging to one of the New York families and the ally who had warned Summer she was in danger. For that alone, we would intervene on Mia's behalf regarding Guido.

I made a point to drop my gaze to his restraints. Both feet were zip-tied to the metal chair, his arms secured behind his back. "What makes you think you can accomplish any of those things? I'm right here." I flashed a malicious grin. "And you haven't managed to harm a hair on my head."

"I won't be here for long. Besides"—his grin was full of entitlement—"you can't do anything to me."

One of the guys snickered behind me. I knew they were enjoying it too. "Because you're the underboss for the Amato family?" I laughed. Damn, he was amusing. "You're not untouchable." I stepped forward, my body angled toward him, then slammed my elbow into his face to make my point. Cartilage crunched under the impact, and his head whipped back from the force of the strike.

Guido straightened so that he was once again glaring daggers at me, despite the steady flow of blood that dripped from his nose. "I'm going to take what you care about most. Today was just a warning."

I saw red. My hands were around his throat. I didn't even remember moving.

His body jerked against the binds, and he gasped for air as I tightened my fingers. His lips turned blue, followed by the skin around his nose and upper lip. I observed him as if from afar. He needed to die. If he didn't, he would go after Hailey again— his threat had been crystal clear.

I felt rather than saw the guys crowd around me. Guido continued to struggle, his body flailing while tethered to the chair. The struggles lessened. He grew weaker. He was close.

Without warning, a hand slammed into my chest. Marco. My fingers loosened, and I glared at my older brother for breaking the killing haze I'd been caught in. Then he pulled one of my hands off Guido's neck. Stefano wrenched the other free.

Outrage fueled me, and I growled my frustration as I strained against their hold. Guido's head slumped forward.

Max pressed his fingers to Guido's pulse at his neck before Marco and Stefano dragged me from the room. The rest of the guys followed. The door shut behind us with a resounding click. I tore my arms free from their grasp. "What the hell?"

"You can't kill him." Stefano's voice was calm and level.

"If I don't, he's going after Hailey." I shoved away from my brother and paced in front of the couch, shoving my hand into my hair and tugging on the short strands.

"Hailey isn't Teresa." Marco's words were quiet.

"I agree with Trey," Nico said as he brought a bottle of whiskey and several glasses from the wet bar.

"Should I get Sof?" Enzo grinned. Total pot-stirrer, but it worked for me.

"Fuck no," Marco growled, running a hand through his black hair.

I laughed, the tension in my shoulders easing. Our sister would have sided with me. Nico handed me a drink, and we all migrated to the sectional, reminiscent of what we used to do when we were growing up—except for Max, who was relatively new to our group, through no fault of his own.

"There are other things at play with Guido." Marco leaned forward, elbows to knees. "Dante will be here in an hour—"

"I thought you just called him." I froze with the drink I'd been about to sip midway to my mouth.

"He was already in the air before any of this went down," Stefano answered, and I swiveled my gaze to our capo.

"Isn't that a little suspect?" Nico topped off his drink, swirling the amber liquid before taking a sip. "He was on his way when Guido happened to attack Trey and Hailey?"

"Things are happening in New York, and killing the Amato underboss isn't going to help," Max said.

I ground my teeth, noticing the pattern. Nico caught my eye and frowned. It was clear the bosses knew what was up. Nico and I were in the dark. "When were we going to learn about this?"

"I'm curious about that too." Nico leaned back, draining the rest of his drink.

Stefano swiped the bottle from the coffee table and refilled his glass. "You know there's unrest among the three New York syndicates. We're meeting with Dante to discuss what he knows and where we might be needed."

"Why would we do that? They're not part of the Five Families." That made little sense. Besides handling Guido and his foot soldier, their problems were not our concern.

"Because the Amato and Tucci families have been strategizing to infiltrate ours," Marco answered then checked his phone. "Dante's jet has landed. He'll be here in half an hour."

"I want in on this meeting." My fingers tightened on the glass. Nico murmured his agreement. We already knew what was going down, and the threats Guido made directly affected me. Marco nodded. It was good he'd agreed, but I would have found a way in even if he hadn't.

Footsteps sounded on the stairs, and all six of us pointed our guns at the stairwell. When Luc reached the basement floor and saw the barrels of our guns aimed at him, he laughed. The newest boss looked like a professional athlete but with light-blue eyes that reflected an age far beyond his years. The amused grin couldn't detract from the old soul that lived inside him or the ruthless predator that would come out if he or any of those he loved were crossed.

As soon as we realized it was Luc, we holstered our weapons. "What are you doing back? I thought you had a few more days in Italy?" Summer had called me before the fiasco with Allen to ask about Braxton Hix contractions. She wasn't that far along, but she'd been reading a pregnancy book and was getting ahead of herself. "Is Summer okay?"

"Yeah." Luc helped himself to a clean glass and splashed two fingers of whiskey in it. "And you've got your dates wrong. We'd planned to come back today. What's going on?"

Max filled Luc in on everything that had happened with Guido. He must not have gone with Summer to the living room, or he would have seen Hailey sitting there with my sister and the other women.

"So we're waiting for Dante before doing anything to Guido?" Luc glanced at the door. "That's bullshit."

"I agree." I stood and bypassed Marco's attempted grab to join Luc behind the door. We would take care of the traitor. There were many things we could do, but at the moment, bullets to the head and heart would satisfy me the most—no need to prolong his life.

Stefano's six-foot-plus frame blocked our way. Dark eyes that spoke of death warned us to tread carefully. "This isn't the time. You'll administer something to knock Guido out for several hours when requested, Trey. That's the only contact either of you will have—for now."

I clenched my fists at my sides, mirroring what Luc was doing. Out of the corner of my eye, I saw Marco glance at his phone before he stood. "Dante's here."

The Verretti boss had arrived to cue us in on the New York syndicate drama and take Guido off our hands. It was time to get that shit show on the road.

CHAPTER EIGHTEEN

TREY

Dante Verretti was in our family's home, and I wasn't entirely comfortable with that, but I told myself to make the best of it. The goal was to take care of Guido so that he was six feet under, sooner rather than later. Stefano had said Dante had a plan.

It had better be a damn good one.

The other bosses, Nico, and I were scattered on the overly large leather sectional when Marco came downstairs with Dante in tow. I sized up the New York boss. His tailored suit was Armani—nice clothes to shield the monster that lurked beneath. Unusual eyes, more gray than green, observed the room, and the way he moved gave the impression that no detail was too small to escape his notice. I caught a glimpse of tats creeping past his collar. Violence radiated from him, despite his outer calm—Dante fit in with us. He had the same predatory, ruthless demeanor encased in a pretty package that could also be wielded as a weapon. I had yet to dissect his personality, although he lacked Guido's smarmy air, so there was hope.

When he joined us on the couch, Marco handed him a drink —none of us wanted to stray far from where we held Guido captive. Introductions were made. Even though we all knew who he was, not everyone had met face-to-face before.

"Why keep Guido alive?" I wasn't wasting time, even though I was out of line speaking before the bosses. They let it slide—though I refused to let my gaze dart to Stefano. He was the only one I really had to worry about.

Luc tensed beside me. A faint crack sounded before he set his glass down. I didn't bother to check to see whether there was a hairline fracture. We all knew there was. "I'm with Trey," he said, his deep voice layered with barely contained violence.

It wouldn't take much to tip him over the edge. The longer we stayed there with Guido on the other side of the door while Summer and Hailey—two targets on Guido's list—were upstairs, the closer we both came to busting into the other room and ending the underboss.

"You could kill him." Dante shrugged. "But his fate will be far worse if I dump him on his father's doorstep."

"We've already delivered proof to Leo Amato. What's to say he won't let this latest infraction slide?" Marco asked.

I knew what the bosses—not Luc, but the rest—were doing. Dante had to be tested. They may have respected him, to a degree, but he needed to prove that his plan was worthwhile for us to go along with it. New York was his city, even if there wasn't an official ruling Mafia family there, and Guido had slipped past his nose as well as all the others'. That didn't fill me with confidence.

"It's simple," Dante said. "Leo knows his place. Once I dump his son on his doorstep with a message that if Guido ever goes to Chicago again, the Five Families will kill him in a way that will go down in history and he will receive the same treatment. He'll have to listen. Leo will have no choice but to put a short leash on Guido."

"There's unrest in the Amato household," Stefano said. "With

Ben's betrayal, Leo would be smart not to test the loyalty of those in his employ."

"Is he smart?" I had my doubts.

Dante grinned, but the gesture lacked warmth. "Smarter than his son. Let them crumble from within."

"We need to help it along. Guido's returned to his family once before after a visit with us. The torture and injury to his hands weren't enough," Nico pointed out.

"Let's deliver another permanent message," Max said. "We'll shave his head and tattoo 'rat' on the side of it."

I laughed. "That'll make a statement. And until his hair grows back, it'll be a constant reminder to Leo about what his son's intentions are to the family."

"Just as a warning"—Enzo rested his arm across the back of the couch—"Guido mentioned something about Mia."

"Mia Tucci?" Dante's brows furrowed.

"Yes," Enzo answered. "He wasn't clear about what he wanted from her, but I can't imagine it's anything good."

"With him, it rarely is."

"Have you found her?" Nico asked.

Dante shoved a hand through his hair, worry pulling at the corners of his mouth.

"No. But we're looking."

The subject was dropped, and the focus returned to our guest just beyond the door. Marco went to the locked closet behind the bar, where we kept instruments and weapons specific to the room Guido was enjoying. He returned with the tattoo machine and supplies, including a folding table with straps. We would have to strap him down and secure his hands, legs, and head so that the process would go smoothly. Rather than sit around and waste time, we filed into the room where Guido was held, and Max got to work.

After Guido was strapped to the table, his mouth duct taped and one side of his head shaved and sterilized, Max outlined the word on his head then used a wider shader needle for fill work rather than one of the liners. Honestly, it was kind of him.

Max guided the needle in bold lines. Like a sewing machine, the needles moved rapidly up and down, depositing ink just beneath Guido's skin.

When he was done, the word "rat" stretched from Guido's temple in large, bold letters. Even when his hair grew back, the R would be visible—the brand would never be fully hidden. I administered a sedative after Max finished the tattoo, and Dante unstrapped Guided then handed him over to one of his guards waiting outside. With our business concluded, they were gone before Hailey or anyone else saw him.

We were nearing dinner, but I didn't want to hang around anymore. Something told me that Hailey and Sofia might have cooked up a plan that I wouldn't like. I'd left her with my sister and the others before our discussion had been settled—well, it had been on my part, but I wasn't blind to the anger brewing on hers. There would be repercussions. And she would probably get whiplash when I told her there was no way I was letting her out of my sight now, even though I'd tried to make her leave before. If I let her walk away, she was at a greater risk than she was by my side, given how Guido wanted to hurt me through her. I couldn't—*wouldn't*—let that happen.

I led the way into the living room, the guys on my heels. I spotted her between my sister and Emiliana on the couch. El, Lil, and Summer were scattered on the other armchairs. All but Summer had a glass of wine. The sight of Hailey hit me hard. She was beautiful, but I'd known that. What struck me in that moment was how she fit with me—and my family. I could see it clear as day. And at that moment, I realized there was no way I could ever let her go.

"Hey." I went over to her, prepared to grovel if need be because there was no way she wasn't angry with me, especially with the rest of them egging her on. I suppressed a shudder at what they could have advised she do. My family was creative. "Let's go."

Her lips pressed into a line, and she did that chin-tilt thing—sexy as hell, but it spelled trouble. I said our goodbyes while practically lifting Hailey to her feet and locking her to my side. Sofia followed us to the front door.

"What's the rush?" Mischief swirled in my sister's eyes.

"Stay out of it, Sof."

She winked at Hailey, and I couldn't stop cringing. They had obviously talked about retaliation. Not good.

Sof grabbed her mane of wavy chestnut hair, swept it to one side, then tossed an envelope my way. I snatched it out of the air. My name was on the label, nothing else.

"That was delivered through a service for you. It just came."

I frowned. I wasn't expecting anything. "Was it checked out?"

She rolled her eyes. "Of course. Security scanned it. It's not a bomb."

I hugged Sof then practically shoved Hailey into her coat.

"Thanks for everything, Sofia." Hailey grinned, and I swore I saw my punishment in that smile. "I'll talk with you later."

Before I second-guessed myself and questioned them about what they'd discussed, I ushered Hailey through the door and into the car.

"Where are we going?"

"Home." I exited the driveway and turned onto the road, pointing us in the direction of the highway.

"You're taking me to my house?"

"No." The sky was dark, the thick, white clouds hidden from view. The days were short, with sunset coming too soon. "I'm sorry about earlier. I was afraid of anything happening to you if you were by my side. But after the incident with Guido, it's clear it's more dangerous if you aren't with me."

"I can take care of myself. Take me home."

"Even if it was safe, Hailey"—I looked away from the road

long enough for her to see the sincerity behind my words—"I want you with me, whether you're in danger or not."

"Then what was that bullshit about staying away from me earlier? I'm not Teresa, and I'm not innocent."

I chuckled, loving that she thought she was a badass. In a way, she was. "I was trying to keep you safe, even if it was from myself. We'll talk more about what was going through my head, promise. But right now, I just want to get you back to the townhouse."

She leaned back in her seat, and we made the rest of the trip to my place on the lake in silence. After we arrived and took the elevator to our floor, my stomach was growling. "I'm going to heat something up. Are you hungry?"

"I could eat." She wandered over to the living room, sat in front of her laptop, and flipped open its lid. I tossed the package on the table next to her then went into the kitchen and heated some pasta for us and poured the wine. I took the whole meal over to where she was and set a plate in front of her. She pushed the computer aside to eat.

I inhaled my food, preparing to have a lengthy chat about earlier when the small package Sofia had given me caught my attention. I snagged it from the coffee table and tore the edge of the padded envelope open. Inside was a small USB stick that could be connected to a phone on one end and a computer on the other. I turned the envelope around to check the front to see who it was from. There was no return address. Rather than getting my computer, I grabbed the laptop Hailey had been working on and plugged in the small drive.

Hailey leaned over to where I sat on the couch. I opened the file and clicked play as a sick feeling settled in my stomach. The image that appeared on the screen was Allen lying on his side on a bed, a sheet—thankfully—covering his lower half. He was naked from the waist up. The camera angle cut off where another person was most likely in a mirrored pose.

"That's not Mom's room. Or any place in the house." Disgust laced her words. "Why do you have this?"

"It came in the mail. And I suspect it's not your mom lying next to him. It's probably a mistress, and I would guess they're in a hotel. I'll send this to Nico later and see if he can place which one." I hit the volume button and turned it up. Even then, the words weren't loud. Allen's were recorded, but hers—whoever the hidden person was—were not. Instead, subtitles were used.

Unknown: *Won't you have to involve the police?*

"No. The threat of doing so will cause harm. It makes sense that I don't."

Unknown: *But you want to involve Trey La Rosa? Isn't that dangerous?*

Allen grinned. It was pure evil. "Of course it is. She's a thorn in my side, and I want her taken care of."

Unknown: *What do you mean, "taken care of"? I thought you wanted her returned unharmed. That's why you didn't contact the police.*

A dark chuckled erupted from the laptop's speakers. "I want her killed."

The video abruptly cut off, and shocked silence filled the void. Anger rumbled deep inside me, and at that moment, I clasped Hailey's trembling hand and decided we were going to take the ransom thing to a whole new level.

CHAPTER NINETEEN

HAILEY

Allen wants me dead. I'd always known he didn't like me. The feeling was mutual, but I just couldn't process him wanting me murdered.

Dark spots converged on the edge of my vision, and another tremor swept through my body. I held on to Trey's hand like a lifeline as I battled warring emotions—first, shock and disbelief, then acceptance, and finally, white-hot fury with a deep-seated need for vengeance.

I would make him pay.

Trey squeezed my hand, effectively yanking me from my thoughts and jolting me back to my surroundings.

My rapid breathing slowed, and I picked through my thoughts. I was in shock. I knew that if Trey wanted to kill me, I would have been dead a long time ago. And he would not have pursued a relationship with me. That wasn't even a concern, but Allen's intentions were, along with anyone else he may have involved. I locked on to Trey, needing the assurance that he would keep me safe. "Allen had to have hired someone."

"It's possible." He stood then closed the distance between us and grasped my shoulders. "Even if he did, I won't let anything happen to you."

He was so close, and I needed to connect to someone. Other than Justin, I had no one and was starved for physical touch from the revelation of how little I meant to the people—and I was including my mom in this fucked-up scenario—who were supposed to care about me. I gave in, knocked his hands off my shoulders, and took a step to eliminate the space between us. I wound my arms around his neck and lay my cheek on his chest, shivering at the way my body responded to his. I didn't have to wait for him to wrap his arms around my waist and pull me close.

He held me for several minutes. I listened to the beat of his heart and felt the even rise and fall of his chest, working to match mine to them. The panic attack dissipated, and my body relaxed into his. When I pulled back, embarrassed by what I'd done, I caught sight of his dilated pupils. My heart rate kicked up another level as he bent his head slowly, giving me time to pull away. I didn't want to.

The first brush of his lips was like a drug, and I parted for him. He drank me in, deepening the kiss and setting my body on fire. The world spun, then time stopped, and there was only him and the intoxicating way he made me feel.

His hand was buried in the back of my hair, cupping my head as he devoured me. He was my oxygen until the frantic rhythm of the kiss slowed and became more sensual, and I moaned at its decadence. When he broke our connection, I gasped. Dazed, I clung to him like a lifeline.

Trey

I hadn't wanted to break the kiss with Hailey. There was nothing better than the feeling of her full lips on mine or the softness of her skin, but I would not take advantage of her. When I made love to her, I wanted all of her invested, not part of her mind reeling in shock.

With the pad of my thumb, I traced her lower lip. She had no idea how stunning she was with her sensual almond-shaped eyes, high cheekbones, and full lips. I loved everything about her, from her wavy dark hair to her slender body that fit perfectly against mine. And I especially loved her nerdy side.

As I gazed at her upturned face, raw vulnerability and unfiltered desire flashed over her features. We would need to talk, but there was no resisting her when she looked at me that way. My need for her raged. The vanilla and strawberry scent from her shampoo teased my senses. All of my self-control snapped. I slanted my mouth over hers, unable to resist the temptation.

When her lips parted, I deepened the kiss, tasting heaven. I gripped her hips and lifted her. She wrapped her legs around my waist while clinging to my shoulders. Desperate for more, I trailed kisses down her jawline. With a small pinch of my teeth on her sensitive neck, she dropped her head back, giving me greater access. Long strides took us to the couch. I teased, sucked, and bit the curve of her neck. She moaned her pleasure. With her legs repositioned to either side of mine, I guided her hips forward, and we both moaned at the friction.

I needed more.

I wanted all of her.

Hailey didn't know it yet, but I was never letting her go.

When her hands tugged at my shirt, her fingers struggled to undo the buttons. I gripped the shirt and pulled. Buttons flew in all directions, bouncing off the floor and rolling to God knew where. The offensive shirt was off in seconds, and her hands roamed across my shoulders and chest then dove into my hair as her mouth crashed into mine in a soul-searing kiss.

With one hand, I cupped her ass, urging her to move faster, and I ground against her core. I trailed my palm over her back to the hem of her shirt, slipping my fingers beneath the material. Her skin was as soft as silk, and I groaned from the sensation of touching her. I skimmed her flat stomach then brushed against the underside of her breast.

Her fingers tightened in my hair, and I cupped her breast, rolling her nipple through the fabric of her bra. She gasped then ground harder against me, and I swear I saw stars from the waves of pleasure having her in my arms gave me.

I could have taken her there and then. It wasn't the time. She was worth waiting for.

Breaking the kiss, I rested my forehead against hers, holding her hips in place so she couldn't move, as our labored breaths gradually regulated.

It took a few minutes for me to gain a semblance of control. "I want you. Just not like this. Not after what you just learned."

When her body relaxed, I pulled her into my embrace. It was late, and we both needed sleep. I stood with her in my arms, and her legs slid down until her feet dangled. As I lowered her, I cursed the way my body raged for every inch of hers. It was going to be a long night.

She wouldn't have said it, but I knew she didn't want to be alone. With her hand in mine, I lead her to my bedroom. "Stay with me. Nothing has to happen. I just want to hold you in my arms tonight."

At her nod, she left to change into clothes to sleep in, and I stripped down to my black boxer briefs. When she returned, I pulled back the covers, and we climbed in. I drew her close, and she snuggled against me. With her head on my shoulder, I stroked her back in a slow circular motion. Her body was relaxed, but knowing her mind, it was nothing but chaos over the news of her stepfather plotting her murder.

"We'll find out who did this"—her body shuddered in my arms—"and if you want, I'll make whoever did pay."

CHAPTER TWENTY

HAILEY

Several days later...

After that first night, I never went back to my bed. Trey and I hadn't had sex yet, but neither of us could resist much longer. And while I appreciated the fact that he didn't take advantage of my messed-up state of mind the other night, I didn't want to wait. I was ready.

For the first time, I trusted a man to want me for myself and not to use me for his agenda. I still needed to get my own place, though, and I'd tried to bring it up to Trey several times, but he'd changed the subject.

I wasn't sure why he thought someone would be after me. That Guido guy was back in New York, and from what Trey had said, he shouldn't be a problem any longer. Part of me wanted to let it go and just stay with him, but we hadn't defined our relationship. And because of that, I wasn't entertaining the idea of living there long term. Things would blow over. They had to. I couldn't fathom any more life-shattering events occurring.

I blew on my coffee and grinned at Trey, who took my empty plate from the island, rinsed it, and put it in the dishwasher. We'd just had breakfast together. I'd cooked, and he insisted on cleaning up while I drank another cup of coffee. He looked incredible in a charcoal-gray cashmere sweater and black pants. His hair was messily rumpled from when I'd run my fingers through it while he'd kissed me senseless. The only reason we'd stopped was that the bacon was burning. It was crispier than I liked but a worthy sacrifice.

Trey's phone buzzed next to me with an incoming text, and I leaned over to peek at the screen. "Sofia's coming up."

He finished putting everything back the way it was in the kitchen then got another cup of coffee for himself as well. "So much for a lazy morning." He followed his words with a wink.

There was no mistaking how close they were. Sofia was a blast. I was curious why she was stopping by, but I hoped it would drag us out of the condo. I could use a distraction from wanting to jump Trey while I knew he was trying to give me space. The funny thing was, I didn't need it. My head was fine, at least as much as it could be after learning Allen wanted to kill me.

I swiped the screen on my phone, revealing the message I'd gotten. Nico had texted. The account of Allen's that we'd watched had been drained right before closing yesterday. All in cash. *What is Allen planning?*

The elevator doors opened with a soft swoosh, and Sofia stepped out, decked in knee-high brown leather boots, tight black pants, and a luxurious-looking tan sweater. She looked gorgeous. "Hey, guys. I came to brighten your day."

Trey got up and hugged her just as my phone rang. It was my mother. I'd given her assistant my new contact info the other day. Mom's PA, Joselyn, managed everything for her, from adding and deleting new contacts into her phone to RSVPing to all the functions she went to and everything in between. I reluctantly accepted the call. Mom calling wasn't usually anything good—usually a demand or a guilt trip to attend whatever charity function she was spearheading.

"Hello, Mother."

"Hailey." Her voice was unusually pitched, and my body automatically went on alert. "Allen is dead."

"What? How could that be?" A flash of when I'd learned my dad and sister had died in a fatal car crash invaded my mind, and pain knifed through my chest, making it difficult to breathe. "What happened?" My voice sounded strained and breathy, and dark spots swam at the edge of my vision. *Please let it have been a heart attack.* As weird as that was, I didn't think I could handle another death by car accident.

Trey was at my side, his fingers curling around mine, but I shook him off. *It's Mom,* I mouthed, leaning away so I could focus, though his proximity managed to clear the dark spots threatening unconsciousness. I was fully alert once more.

"He was found in his car."

My heart skipped a beat then raced frantically. "An accident?"

"An exhaust leak."

"Wait. That doesn't make sense. He had a new Audi."

Mom huffed. "I can't be bothered with the details. There was a hole somewhere, and it leaked into the car. He died in the parking lot at the hospital this morning."

"You saw him before?"

"Of course I did." Her voice pitched up another octave, reflecting her annoyance with me. I was very familiar with that tone.

I squeezed my eyes shut and rubbed my forehead, but it did no good. I was as confused as ever. "Allen wouldn't have killed himself." He was a selfish ass and as narcissistic as my mother. There wasn't a depressed or self-sabotaging bone in his body.

"I never said he did," she snapped. "I called to tell you. The funeral is in two days. I expect you to wear the black Armani in your closet. I cannot believe I have to dress in black. You know how it washes me out."

"Then wear something else." Dealing with my mother was exhausting.

"Don't be absurd. And, Hailey."

"Yes?" I slumped over the island, weary with her brand of crazy.

"Don't embarrass me by being late or failing to show up."

Three beeps sounded. *Unbelievable.* She'd hung up.

"What happened?"

Trey's deep voice startled me, and I jumped, lifting my head from the island's cool marble countertop. So wrapped up in the call from my mom, I'd forgotten Trey and Sofia were in the room with me. They were both frowning, and Trey's expression was fiercer and more protective than curious.

I waved my hand over the phone then swiveled to face them. "That was my mom. She called to tell me that Allen is dead."

"You said something about suicide?" Concern swam in Sofia's warm brown eyes, replicas of her brother's.

"It seemed that way when she'd said he died from exhaust inhalation, but that doesn't make sense. For one, Allen would never kill himself. And he would have smelled the exhaust and refused to drive the car."

"Are you all right?" Trey's hand rested on my shoulder.

"Yeah, it's just a shock." I tried to smile, but it was weak at best. "Well, I don't have anything to worry about from him any longer."

Trey squeezed my shoulder before dropping his hand. "Let me make a few calls. I'll see what I can find out about what went wrong with his car and whether it was tampered with."

After Trey left to investigate in his office, Sofia led me to the couch. "Are you sure that you're okay? Can I get you anything?"

"No. I mean, I'm fine. I don't need anything." I worried my

lower lip with my teeth, debating what to do. "I need to make a call."

"Do you want me to give you some privacy?"

I shook my head. "It's fine. I'm just going to try to reach a friend of mine. He's been hard to get ahold of lately." *You'd better pick up, Justin.*

Sofia pulled out her phone and started to scroll through her emails while I pressed the contact button for Justin. It rang three times. I leaned my head back against the couch, resigned to talking to his voicemail.

"Hello?"

Justin's familiar voice snapped me back to the call. "You answered!"

"Hailey? What's wrong?"

"What's wrong?" I laughed, and Sofia's gaze jerked my way. I avoided looking at her because even I'd heard how deranged I sounded. "You've ghosted me." Fury colored my words, and I was more than fine with him hearing the emotion. "I don't care that you told Allen. I know why you did. *I know you.* But not taking my calls…"

"I'm sorry." It was quiet. Heartfelt.

All my pent-up aggression fizzled but didn't dissipate completely. "You're forgiven. For that. But I'm still mad, and I need you to go somewhere with me."

"Okay?"

I welcomed that edge of snarkiness. I wanted things to go back to normal between us, but they wouldn't yet. I tried to bridge the gap from my anger at him to what mattered deep down. "I've missed you."

"How could you not?"

"Snot." But he got me to laugh, and I was grateful for that. "Allen's dead. The funeral is in two days, and I'll have to deal with Vanessa. Please go with me."

"Back up. Allen's dead? What happened?"

"She said it was an exhaust leak, but that just seems suspect."

"Why? It's either a car malfunction or a suicide, right?"

"That's what I thought, but we both know Allen would never take his own life."

"You think someone sabotaged the car? Wouldn't the police have figured that out?"

I shoved my hair away from my face. "Yes, and I hear what you're saying. Still, it's weird, right?"

"Very." He paused for a beat. "Maybe Trey had something to do with it?"

I pushed off the back of the couch and stood, pacing as his harebrained idea took root. "No, Trey would never." But he was Mafia. It would have been so easy. Trey walked back into the room, a hard glint in his eyes, and I paused my pacing. "I've got to go. And for the record, I'm furious with you. You and I are going to have it out. What you're doing isn't okay. We've been through this same scenario before, and I'm not having it, Justin." I had to take a calming breath. He made a strangled noise on his end, and I could practically see him rolling his eyes. I knew what that sound was—he'd bit back a snide retort. My guess was that he actually understood the gravity of the situation I'd brought to his attention, because Justin did not like being called out for his bullshit ghosting ways. "I'll call you later with the funeral details."

We said goodbye, then I rounded on Trey, my hands shaking with barely restrained emotion. "What did you do?"

He stiffened. "I didn't do anything, Hailey. I was with you all night. He died this morning."

I pointed at him, unable to stop myself. My emotions were going haywire from not being able to have it out with Justin in the way we both had needed, and they were misdirected. But I couldn't stop myself. "You could have had someone tamper with the car for you. And the fact that you knew what I was talking about says everything."

Trey frowned, and Sofia jumped up, blocking my view of him.

"Let's calm down." She grabbed my hand, the one that was pointing an accusing finger at him. "Trey, I'm taking Hailey to the gun range. Okay?" She didn't wait for a response but started herding me to the elevator, grabbing coats from the front closet. "Meet up with us later."

I was too stunned by Sofia's shoving to react. It didn't help that my mind was in absolute chaos. I clamped my mouth shut and went with it. The elevator doors closed, but not before I caught a glimpse of Trey's fierce glower. Remorse was late in coming. *What have I done?* After everything that man did for me, I treated him like an enemy.

I grabbed Sofia's arm. "I've got to go back."

She laughed then shook her head and dragged me to her waiting car. "Nope. We're going to the range. I'll make calls in the car and see who can meet us there."

I let her push me into the passenger seat and take me away from Trey. Maybe it was for the best. I needed to get my head on straight before I went back and said some additional messed-up thing to him. Because I wasn't entirely sure he didn't have a hand in Allen's death.

Allen was a pompous asshat, but killing him hardly seemed fair.

And if Trey did have Allen killed, I wasn't sure I would be able to get past it.

HAILEY

I fell silent as Sofia raced along the highway at breakneck speed. Soon, she took one of the exits then pulled into a parking lot. I stared straight ahead at a looming warehouse-like structure as several other vehicles arrived in the spots surrounding us. I guessed the SUVs were security.

"Hey." Sofia squeezed my arm. "Everything is going to be okay. I called in a few of the girls. We're hitting the range and blowing off some steam. It'll be fun. I promise. 'Kay?"

I managed a weak smile. "Sure."

She pushed the door open and got out of the car. I was slower to react, my body feeling like it'd been tenderized from watching the video of Allen plotting my death, worrying about Justin, hearing of Allen's actual death, dealing with my mom, and being targeted by a New York mafia underboss. It was a lot to process in a short span of time.

Several car doors opened and closed. I didn't pay much attention until Emiliana and El swung into view. I worked harder to shove my crappy mood aside and said hello.

"Wow." El pulled me in for a hug. "You've had a morning."

Sofia snorted. "Let's do this."

El released me, and I fell into step beside Emiliana as Sofia and El led us toward the massive building. The only windows were on the glass front doors. The rest of the structure was some sort of dark-gray sheet metal. Their security went in front and behind us with several at the side, forming a diamond of protection. Once inside and closing in on the front desk, we were waved through by the guys sitting there.

"We don't come here often, but when we do, there a few private ranges set aside for our use," Emiliana explained.

We weaved through the hallways until we came to a locked door. One of the security guys opened it, and we filed in while the guards remained in the hallway. Some had stayed in the lobby and a few more were outside the entrance. The shooting bays were divided by plexiglass, and electric panels were mounted to the side of each unit that must have had the ability to move the targets.

Sofia pulled a gun from her purse. It looked like a 9mm, but I honestly had no idea. El and Emiliana did the same, along with a few clips or magazines. It was pretty basic stuff, but I'd never been around guns before. I just hadn't paid attention to what the specific parts of a gun were called. And until that day, I'd never cared to learn.

Sofia wrapped her arm around me and led me to one of the bays. She handed me noise-canceling headphones but stopped me before putting them on.

"This is what you're going to do." She positioned the gun in my hand. "Hold it like this." I demonstrated how the grip should be between the webbing of her thumb and index finger. Three fingers wrap around the base of the grip and below the trigger guard. The thumb rests along the frame. Then her index finger only goes on the trigger when she's ready to shoot. "Look down the sight. Line up the top sight with the rear, point, and shoot. It's a great way to get your frustrations out." She winked then flicked her long, wavy ponytail over her shoulder. "Trust me."

She put on a pair of headphones when I did then leaned against the plexiglass as I followed her instructions. I fired off a few shots then lowered the gun. Sofia made a rolling motion to keep going with her finger. So I did. I channeled all the frustration, aggression, and fear I'd felt in the past few days and kept firing until there were no more bullets. When I handed over the gun, she popped part of it off and reloaded it. Then she hit a button on the control panel, and the target I was aiming for moved forward until it stopped a foot from where we stood.

"Look." She grinned. "You got a few on the sheet."

My cheeks burned. "On the edge of the paper." If that had been a person and I had to shoot him in a life-or-death situation, I would have been the one bleeding out. Not a single shot had hit the actual silhouette.

El poked her head into our space and checked out my dismal attempt to hit the target. "You're learning. Don't worry about it."

Emiliana joined us, taking her headphones off and letting them hang around her neck. "You'll get the hang of it. You hit the target. Be proud of that."

"Besides, we'll teach you." El grinned. "And speaking of you being around… what's going on between you and Trey?"

Sofia's nose scrunched up. "Please keep it PG."

"It's pretty PG. Don't worry." I worked hard to keep the longing from my voice. I wanted more, which told me the accusation I'd made was most likely off base—I was a decent judge of character. "After I blamed him for having something to do with my stepfather's death, I don't think there's anything more to it. He'll probably happily drop me at home after this."

Sofia snorted. "He's not going to get rid of you. Trust me. The way my brother looks at you says it all."

"I've got to agree with Sof," Emiliana said. "Trey's never acted like he does with you."

"Not even when he was dating Teresa." El leaned against the plexiglass. "He only *thought* he was into her."

"True. She was a temporary vacation from his life, which he needed with everything that was going on." Sofia's expression sobered. "It wasn't easy for him to graduate high school so early. He went to college at fifteen. My brother's a genius. Imagine what that was like… and then to push himself to excel in med school and during his residency, all the while maintaining what the family expected of him."

"We've talked about dating," I confessed, needing to get more clarity on the situation from their perspectives. "I'm just worried he'll lose interest once all the danger with Guido is over."

"You're referencing that bullshit about sending you home the other day?" Emiliana frowned. "Take it from all of us—they try to push us away until they can't deny their feelings any longer. It's like this weird white-knight act they try on in the name of us being safer without them. It's a load of bullshit. They can't deny the monsters inside them, and honestly, I wouldn't have it any other way." She shrugged, and the other two nodded, wearing knowing sinister grins.

"His denial of his feelings won't last." El chuckled. "Well, for you, it didn't even last half a day. Must be the genius in him." She winked at Sofia.

"He's still an idiot. All men are." Sofia rolled her eyes. "But we love them anyway."

"This idiot is ready to take Hailey away before you corrupt her any further." Trey stood with a wide stance inside the door, arms crossed over his chest.

"See what I mean?" Sofia glared at Trey then pulled me in for a tight hug. "We'll do this again. You're good for him. Don't give up the fight." That last part was whispered.

I squeezed her back. I hugged Emiliana and El, then handed over the equipment I was using before joining Trey. "How much of that did you hear?"

"Enough."

He opened the door, and we exited. As soon as it shut behind us, he put his hand on my lower back. I couldn't suppress the full-body shiver from his touch.

"I'm sorry." The words were soft, but he turned my way as if he'd heard me.

"I won't kill someone in your family without good reason or you knowing about it, and certainly not like that."

We navigated the parking lot, and I climbed into a black Range Rover that must have been one of his cars. He got behind the wheel and pulled out to the street. We had much to discuss, mostly my accusing him of killing Allen when the problem was that I was hurt, confused, and lashing out. He just happened to be my scapegoat, thanks to the little seed of doubt Justin had planted.

He weaved through cars then took the ramp to get onto the highway. We were headed in the direction of his condo. I wasn't sure I was ready to go back there.

"I heard you on the phone. What I'm assuming Justin said to get you to believe I would have had Allen's car tampered with."

I bit my lower lip, not trusting myself to say anything. Part of me felt defensive, protective of my friend. But Trey didn't deserve my reaction.

"If you have doubts or questions, please bring them to me before jumping to conclusions."

That was a reasonable request. "I will." A weight fell from my shoulders. I toyed with a strand of my hair, twisting it around my finger then releasing it, only to repeat the movement all over again. "I shouldn't have lashed out at you like that. I'm struggling to process anything. And Justin ghosting me during this time has been difficult. I get why, but it doesn't make it any easier."

"Do you want to swing by his place?" Trey threaded my hand with his, pulling both over to rest on his firm thigh. "Talk it out with him before the funeral?"

"I do." It would go a long way if Justin and I could hash things out. I'd sensed the distance in his tone when we'd spoken over the phone, and I didn't like it. He was overly sensitive. I understood that about him, but he was taking things too far lately. It needed to stop.

We fell into silence with Trey stroking the back of my hand now and again. He could have been a major ass about what I'd said earlier, and the fact that he hadn't been went a long way to soothe some of my fears about getting involved with him. Not physically—I was insanely attracted to him. But the world he came from... I thought I fit, but there were moments when I wasn't sure.

We pulled up in front of Justin's brick bungalow, and I scanned for his car. I didn't see it, but that didn't mean he wasn't home. He could have had trouble finding a parking spot on the crowded street. Trey double-parked. His security was behind us. They would handle any issues that arose from blocking the way.

We hurried up the steps as an arctic wind tore down the street. I shivered as I pounded on the front door. His doorbell had been broken for a good six months. He'd never bothered to get it fixed. When the door didn't open, I fished out the key with fingers that were losing their feeling. Trey took the key from my shaking hand and opened the lock. He shut the door behind us, and we stomped off any snow from walking through the parkway.

"Justin!" I wandered through the house. The kitchen looked the same as it had the last time we were there.

"Is he usually home at this time?"

"Typically." I hurried down the basement steps. There was no sign of life there either. We retraced our path then went upstairs. In his bedroom, I began to worry. Things were missing—clothes, bathroom products, and all his shoes.

I shed my coat, a sheen of perspiration coating my upper lip and hairline. *Why is it so hot in here?* I hadn't noticed it before, as it was an icebox outside, and I'd needed the warmth when we'd entered.

I couldn't suppress the panic any longer and turned to face Trey. "He's gone. I don't understand." I wrung my hands, not knowing how to contain my worry. "He took his shoes."

Trey went over to the thermostat and played with the button. After about a minute of messing with it, he stopped. "The heat's broken. It's hot as hell in here. I'm sure he went to stay somewhere else, a hotel maybe, until it's fixed."

"No. He wouldn't do that. It's too expensive."

"Then a friend's." He tugged on my hand. "Come on. Let's get out of here."

We rushed down the stairs and out the door. I almost welcomed the cold air. When we were back in the car, I tried Justin's phone again, but it went to voicemail. I left a message, relaying the details for the funeral and asking where he was. After I hung up, I couldn't shake the feeling that something was very wrong.

CHAPTER TWENTY-TWO

HAILEY

I had time to think in the car on the way to the condo. The rollercoaster of emotions and lashing out at Trey had to end. I was better than that, and he deserved more from me. I isolated what I was feeling to one emotion: fear for Justin. In my heart, I knew something was wrong. Maybe none of it was even about me—maybe he and his boyfriend had broken up or were fighting. I hadn't been around to confide in, so I didn't know. I hated what was happening between us and had to get it resolved. After the funeral, I planned to confront him face-to-face, and we could put all the weirdness in the past, where it belonged.

With my mind made up, took a deep breath then let all of it go. Everything would work out. It always did.

After Trey parked, we took the elevator to his living space. Once inside, I kicked off my boots and hung up my coat, watching him go straight for the wine. He took down two glasses, poured red in each, then held one out for me to take. I accepted it, standing closer than was usual, and took a sip. But that wasn't what I wanted. "I know we need to talk, and I'm sorry again for the way I acted."

Trey ran a hand through his hair, and indecision showed in his taut features. I needed to take control of the conversation before it started.

"Even though we need to, I don't want to talk."

"You don't?" His brows furrowed, and he set his glass on the island next to mine. His gaze flitted from my eyes to my lips, reading my intent before I made a move.

I closed the distance between us and placed my hands on his firm chest, trailing my fingers until they settled on his incredible biceps. I loved how strong he was, mentally and physically. A thrill of excitement about what I was initiating raced through me as his hands went to my hips. He tugged me to him, and I went willingly. "I want you. All of you. Nothing is holding me back." We'd been interrupted too many times when things between us heated up, either from circumstances or his iron will. I wasn't having it, and I made my intent clear.

His hand slid up to bury his fingers at my nape, the other firm at my hip. Desire swirled in his eyes, dilating his pupils. My lips parted as he slowly dipped his head, giving me time to pull away. That wasn't happening. I wanted him badly.

I rose to my toes and brushed my mouth over his, winding my arms around his neck. He took control of the kiss, coaxing me to open and teasing my tongue with his. Heat quickly built between us, and I melted into him. His gentle pulling on my hair sent sparks of need all the way to my toes. I moaned into his mouth. He urged my hips closer.

I tugged on the silky strands of his hair, needing more as he took command of my mouth and my body. He gripped my hips and lifted me onto the island. I grasped his shoulders, suddenly desperate to get rid of the barrier of clothing between us as his muscles rippled under my hands.

I fumbled with the buttons on his shirt, undoing a few. He broke our kiss, took a step back, and removed the offensive item for me. Not wasting a second, I whipped my shirt off, getting momentarily caught in a mass of curls as my hair blocked my view of his chiseled, drool-worthy chest.

He stilled my frantic fingers and gently pushed my hair back. My heart pounded against my ribs as he unhooked my bra and slowly slid the straps from my shoulders then down my arms to join the other items of clothing on the floor. I shivered in the chilly air, and he groaned. His hand cupped my breast, and he rolled my nipple between his fingers while I arched into him, needing more.

"You're beautiful, Hailey." His deep voice rumbled with conviction.

And at that moment, I felt like it.

He swept me into his arms and carried me to the bedroom. His skin on mine made me dizzy with desire. I trailed kisses down his neck and over part of his chest until he gently placed me on his king-sized bed. The curtains were open, and light shone in the room. There was no hiding from his view, and I didn't want to.

He swiftly unzipped his pants, dropped them to the floor, then joined me on the bed in only his tight black boxer briefs. I feasted on him with sight alone. My mouth watered.

I'd never been with anyone who looked like him—a Greek god, only Italian—and who made my blood sing the way he did. Heat flooded my core. I wanted to lick him everywhere—he was so sexy.

"You're overdressed." His voice was rough with desire as he bent to trail kisses along my abdomen, slowly sliding my leggings down. His mouth followed, pressing open-mouth kisses on my exposed skin, and I buried my fingers in his hair.

He nipped the sensitive spot below my hip bone, and I shuddered. The feeling of his lips on my skin was driving me over the edge. I squirmed against him, wanting more. Somehow, my legs were bare. It was magic—I had no idea how that'd happened. My skin heated with his every touch. I gasped when fabric tore, and he whisked my panties off.

When he shifted lower, his hard length brushed against my thigh, and I realized in my lust-hazed state that he'd stripped the remaining clothing from his body. Nothing separated us, and my hands moved restlessly over his shoulders. I needed to touch him and make him lose control as he was with me. Tugging on his hair, I tried to get him to move up so more of him was within reach. He lifted his head, and I gasped at his passion-filled eyes and swollen lips. It struck me deep in my core—he was becoming my world, the air I needed to breathe.

My hypersensitive nerve endings sang as he spread my legs, baring me to his sight. He trailed featherlight caresses up my inner thighs, and I curled my hands in the sheets, desperate for him to touch my throbbing clit.

Sparks sizzled along my skin in the wake of his mouth, his every touch. I'd never experienced anything like the solid and all-consuming connection that built between us.

At the first touch of his mouth, my back arched, and jolts of pleasure flooded my system. I lost track of my surroundings, riding the cresting waves of desire from his skilled mouth and fingers. His teeth nipped gently at my nub while his fingers curled inside me. Our gazes caught, and he flashed me a wicked grin before replacing his fingers with his tongue. I panted, plumping beneath his touch and growing wetter with every caress.

He teased and toyed with me as sensations stacked on top of each other. I couldn't hold out much longer. Heat built, and I squirmed, what I wanted so close. Explosions rocked my body, and I screamed his name. When the last tremor quieted, my body went limp.

When he shifted off me, my skin raised with goose bumps. I heard a wrapper open. And then his body covered mine again. Desire burned in his warm brown eyes. My hand skimmed down his side, reaching to feel the long length and width of him. He captured my wrist and gave a slight shake of his head, his features tightly restrained.

I felt him against my core, and he stilled, his lust-filled gaze holding mine. "You good with this?" His voice was low and husky.

I wrapped a leg around his waist, inviting him in. "Yes." I couldn't manage anything else. I arched against him, my body quivering with need. Then he slowly pushed into me, stretching me to the max. His back was tense beneath my fingers, the corded muscles straining against tight skin. I raised my hips, desperate for him to move.

"You drive me crazy, Hails."

At the intimacy of my shortened name, my body softened even more. A jolt of awareness filled me—I was in love with him. Every part of it felt right. I was meant to be in his arms, walking beside him, his ride-or-die partner for life. And given the way he looked at me, I was pretty sure he felt the same.

He thrust deeply, hitting that magical spot. All thoughts fled, and I gasped at the sensual onslaught. I didn't think anymore—I only felt. When he captured my mouth with his, I held him tightly, the sensations building upon one another. My core tightened. I gripped his biceps, my fingernails digging in as stars burst behind my eyelids, and I screamed in his mouth. He dove into me, each thrust fueling my orgasm, and my body convulsed around him until he whispered my name as he followed me over the edge.

In his embrace, I trembled with the realization that I would never be the same. One time with him would never be enough.

On one elbow, holding the majority of his weight from me, he traced my cheek with his other hand. "This changes things, Hails. You're mine. I can't let you go."

I arched a brow and let a slow, knowing smile curve my lips. "Who said I wanted to go anywhere? You're *mine*."

His laughter, full of promise and joy, warmed me deep in my soul. When he shifted, I shivered from the loss of heat, but he had to take care of the condom. He took a quick trip to the bathroom and returned with a washcloth that he used to clean me. I whimpered as the warm material brushed against my overly sensitive skin. He tossed it in the direction of the bathroom, and the bed dipped from his weight as he lay beside me then gathered me in his arms. I rested my head on his shoulder and tangled my legs with his. There was no place else I wanted to be.

⁂

Trey

Hailey felt right in my bed and in my arms. I might have fooled myself and thought I could let her go before, but what had just happened between us sealed the fact that I never could. She was mine, I was hers, and we both knew it. But there was unfinished business between us, and if we were to make our relationship work, everything needed to be out in the open.

I brushed her wavy hair from her face, loving how the mixture of springy and loose curls attempted to wrap around my fingers every time I touched the silky strands. "We need to talk." I snuggled her more tightly against me.

Her body tensed. "Okay… what about, specifically?"

"I need to be honest with you about something. When I said you should stay here at least until you found something else, I didn't mean it."

With her hand flat on my chest, she tried to push herself away.

I didn't let her. "I never planned on letting you go. I would have found excuses for you to have to remain here with me. This place isn't mine any longer. It's ours."

"You tried to send me away."

"I did. I thought it was for the best. But I realized the way for me to keep you safest was to stop fighting what was between us. I'll protect you with my life."

Her hand flattened on my chest, her body once again relaxing. "I'm not Teresa."

I closed my eyes, regretting ever comparing her to a woman that wouldn't have held a candle to the one in my arms. "I know. But this life is dangerous."

"I'm not hiding anymore."

"What do you mean?"

"Ever since Dad and Kasey died, I've been hiding. Not standing up for myself, not going for what I want—taking a back seat to life. But with you, that all changed. I can be myself."

"I like who you are. I would never want you to change."

"I'm not helpless either. I've taken martial arts. Sure, I barely know how to shoot a gun, but I'll learn."

I chuckled at how fierce she sounded. I had no doubt she would master it—Hailey could do anything. "Do you want to go back to MIT and finish your degree?"

She traced small circles on my chest with the pad of her finger. "No. I should tell you the truth about why I dropped out. It wasn't just because I didn't know what to do with the rest of my life and I felt like I was wasting my time there. I could have majored in several things, and I would have been fine. I liked the classes, and the work was easy enough. I left because of a boy."

She filled me in on what her jackass ex had talked her into doing for him with his grades and how he'd threatened to rat her out to the dean of students.

Anger burned inside me, and the need for vengeance had me seeing red.

"Stop." She reached up and cupped my face. "He isn't important. I don't care about him. He holds no power over me."

He'd hurt her, and I would find a way to make him pay. Maybe not that day, but soon.

"There can be no secrets between us."

I gritted my teeth, knowing she explicitly referred to retaliation against her ex. "I agree." And I would be honest with her about what I was going to do once I figured it out. For the time being, I forced myself to release the tension, focusing on us instead. There was more that I had to share with her. "I think I knew you were the one the moment I laid eyes on you in that basement, unapologetically faking your abduction. I love you, Hailey. And I'll support your decision if I'm moving things too fast and you need to be on your own for a while. You could take the floor below me. But I'm not letting you go."

When she shifted against me, it was to lie on top of me. She met my gaze and held it. "I don't need space. I love you, too, Trey."

CHAPTER TWENTY-THREE

TREY

I weaved through cars on the highway with the sun still rising in the sky and shining into my eyes from the awkward angle, despite my sunglasses. Dante had called Stefano, and the guys were meeting at his house that morning to go over what they'd talked about. I was on my way there after a hurried breakfast with Hailey. We'd stayed in bed too long then had to rush when we realized the time. I couldn't get enough of her body and already missed her by my side. But Allen's funeral was later that day, so I'd dropped Hailey at her mom's with a contingent of security that would ensure her safety from a reasonable distance.

She wanted to do it on her own, saying her mom would be even more difficult if she brought anyone with her before the proceedings. I'd agreed only because I had to go to the meeting and with the assurance that my guards would have eyes on her the entire time. As soon as I was done with my obligations, I planned to head over to where she was. When the funeral was over, she was going to pack some clothes to bring back to our lakefront home.

I pulled off Lake Shore Drive to a greystone similar to mine, where Stefano lived with Emiliana. After entering the code, I gained access to the lower-level parking. Several cars were already there. Once in the elevator, I pressed my hand to the scanner then hit the button for the top floor. It took seconds to arrive, and the doors opened soundlessly.

Emiliana passed me and took my place in the elevator. "Morning, Trey."

"Morning." I raised my eyebrows, wondering where she was off to, but she only grinned and hit the button to close the doors. The guys were all there—both my brothers, Stefano, Luc, Enzo, and Max. None of the Mafia women were, though. "Where's Emiliana off to?" *Are they going to the funeral?*

"She's meeting the girls for brunch. Then they're going to Hailey's to help her pack."

"Why is this the first I'm hearing of that?" My fingers curled around my phone, and I started to pull it from my pocket to text Hailey.

Stefano smirked. "Because your sister just spoke with her about two minutes ago and found out she's moving some of her stuff into your place after the funeral."

"So Hailey's the one?" Marco slapped me on the back. "Nico's the only single guy left?"

"Tony too," Max said.

Marco flinched. I'd forgotten about him too. Tony didn't hang with us much anymore, even though he was Max's brother. "Guess you're not the last man standing, Nic."

Nico chuckled then slapped me on the back before taking a seat on one of the island chairs.

"Yeah," I answered Marco. "Hailey's the one. So let's get this meeting going so I can get back to her."

Enzo grinned but refrained from a smartass comment, which I appreciated. The fact that I still owed him from the misdirection of my brother's focus when he kissed my sister bothered me. I barely suppressed a shudder at that image.

There was coffee on the island, and I helped myself to a cup. "Is Guido still in New York?" That weasel needed to stay the hell away from Hailey.

"From what Dante said, he is." Stefano grabbed coffee, too, then leaned a hip against the counter. The rest of the guys were crowded around the oversized marble island, sitting or standing. "Guido's on lockdown by his father's orders."

"He's at the Amato estate?" Enzo asked.

"From what I understand," Stefano responded. "He's been stripped of his position."

"No longer the underboss." I was only partially satisfied. It was a start. And from the granite cast of Luc's jaw, he felt the same.

"But he's crafty," Marco warned. "We need to watch out in case he slips under the radar without Dante or anyone else knowing. It happened last time, and Leo Amato doesn't know who else in his employ is on Guido's side."

"It's possible that Leo is playing a game of his own," Enzo offered.

"You think he's orchestrating his son's moves?" It wasn't an outlandish thought, but there were holes in his theory.

"Let's see how this plays out," Max said.

"If Guido returns, nothing is stopping me from killing him," Luc growled, daring Stefano to say otherwise.

"Agreed." Stefano shoved his dark-blond hair off his forehead then pushed off the counter. "We have one more concern."

"Mia?" Nico's brows rose.

I thought I'd detected a hint of interest, but that couldn't have been. None of us but Summer had met her.

"Yes," Marco answered. "From what Dante told Stefano, her father is on the warpath to get her back. Dante doesn't like how the Tucci boss is handling things, and if we get wind of where Mia is, he wants us to share the information with him or his brothers only. He's worried about her safety."

Speaking of safety, I could barely contain the urge to race back to Hailey's side. Marco caught Nico and me up on a few other business issues, and when we were done, I got ready to leave. But then Mom called from Italy, and I lost track of time as she regaled me with Vincenzo and Katherine's drama. Katherine was thriving under Vincenzo's attention. We finished the conversation with Mom's update about how Katherine was feeling. I'd gotten a few medical updates, and the treatment was working. Everything was going as I'd hoped it would for Katherine.

By the time I got off the phone, Allen's funeral was over. Emiliana, my sister, and the others would be with Hailey. It was nearing lunch, and Luc was rummaging around in Stefano's fridge. Nico dropped onto the couch next to me, and I knew I wasn't going to be able to leave for a while longer.

I kept telling myself that Hailey was okay and to relax, but my gut said otherwise.

CHAPTER TWENTY-FOUR

HAILEY

"I need to talk to you." I entered the parlor where Mom had coffee mixed with a mystery liquor. She would have denied it if asked, but I was sure her drink was laced.

She turned her head in my direction, and I caught a minuscule flinch when her gaze landed on my face. A stranger wouldn't have noticed, but I had.

We didn't resemble one another. She had honey-blond hair and brown eyes. Kasey had looked more like Mom, especially her hair and eyes. Mine were the exact shade as Dad's, though Kasey and I had always looked like sisters. When Mom looked at me, she saw *them*, which was why she rarely did anymore.

I couldn't blame her. Their absences left a hole in my heart, too, but I chose to go on, to let myself love and be loved. She hadn't. She'd never cared deeply for Allen. He was a plus one to go to events with and nothing more.

Good thing I'd kept the black Armani dress on rather than changing into a pair of jeans and a long-sleeved shirt. Dressing appropriately was important to her, which set me apart from my family. I was a yoga-pants-loving, jeans-and-T-shirt kind of girl, whether I came from money or not. And I did. One would just never have known it.

I sat next to her on the love seat, doing my best to ignore the hideous color scheme in the parlor. She loved the pale-yellow walls and antique floral furniture. I did not and avoided that room at all costs. It was fitting that it was in that space where I was about to tell her I was leaving.

Part of me regretted telling her my news on the day of Allen's funeral, but it would be a gift, in a way. We could both get some relief and a fresh start. She would no longer be burdened by me, her constant reminder of how much she'd lost.

Better to rip the Band-Aid off. "I'm moving out."

"Oh?" It was as if she barely registered my news.

That's it? I'm not even worthy of an ounce of concern, even a question about where I would be living? I didn't know why I expected anything. "Yes. I have some friends coming over to help me pack. It shouldn't take more than a few hours."

I had to stop myself from getting up and just walking out. She was my mom. I owed her compassion even if she didn't show any toward me. "Will you be all right?"

She rose her haughty blond eyebrows, and I had to fight from rolling my eyes.

"Of course. I don't need your presence in this house to function. I have Joselyn."

Her assistant. I wasn't surprised. "Great. Then I'll get to it." I got to my feet as she picked up her coffee, took a sip, then returned her attention to her phone.

As I was leaving the hideous parlor, her faint voice registered: "Be happy, Hailey." I had to stop, my hand coming in contact with the wall on the other side of the room. I braced myself against the onslaught of emotions from Mom's parting words. She didn't show it to my face, but I guess she did care.

Once the majority of my swirling emotions had settled, I pushed off the wall, my steps lighter than they had been in years. Maybe the space would be good for us, and we could salvage some kind of relationship in time.

My phone pinged, pulling me from my thoughts. A glance at the screen told me the message was from Sofia. They had arrived. Rather than bother my mom with the news that my friends were there, I hurried through the house to open the front door for them.

I flung it open just as Summer, El, Emiliana, Lil, and Sofia came up the steps. I leaned into their hugs as they entered the house.

"I would say I'm sorry for your loss," Sofia said with a straight face, "but I'm not."

"Because he wanted me dead?" I could laugh about it now.

She tapped the end of her nose. "That's the main reason. The other is that I never liked him. He was a pompous ass."

I laughed then looked around quickly, ensuring my mom wasn't nearby to hear what Sofia had said or my reaction.

"Where's your room?" El took a few backward steps toward the grand staircase just off the foyer. "Let's get this party started."

All the tension from being there and going to the funeral disintegrated. I waved them in the right direction, and we set off for the back stairs, closest to my room, then made our way up and fanned into the space. Summer plopped down on my bed, kicked her feet up, and sighed as she leaned back.

"This baby needs to come out." She ran a hand over her small baby bump. "I'm constantly hungry and need to go to the bathroom."

"Soon." Lil gave her a side hug then sat beside her. "And I can't wait to hold your baby."

"What are we packing?" Sofia disappeared into my closet with El hot on her heels.

I didn't expect to see them anytime soon, not with how Sofia was with clothes. "There are suitcases in the back corner. Just shove whatever looks good in there." I didn't care that much, and I trusted Sofia. The only things that mattered to me were my sister's candles and my pictures.

Emiliana noticed I was wrapping picture frames in soft T-shirts that I wanted to bring from my dresser in the closet. She came over to help. There were a lot of them. I had a box at my feet.

"How was the funeral?" She picked up a picture of Kasey and me and paused to study it before carefully wrapping it and setting it inside the box.

I was grateful she didn't ask about my sister. For some reason, I didn't want to talk about family. Allen didn't count—I'd never considered him to be part of mine. "It was what I expected, dull and way too long." Justin never showed, which had upset me and shedding a few tears. I didn't know what was going on with that boy, but we were going to have a come-to-Jesus moment the next time I saw him—and that needed to be soon.

"Is your mom doing okay?"

"Yeah." I smiled genuinely. "She is."

Summer moved over so she and Lil could start folding whatever Sofia tossed on the bed before it went into the suitcases. There was a slight crinkling noise, and Summer lifted the pillow just as Trey walked into the room. I ignored what she was doing and went straight into his open arms.

"Hailey," Summer called out. "There's an envelope that was under your pillow. It has your name on it."

"What?" That was weird. Trey released me, and we went over to where she held the envelope for me. My heart sank when I saw the familiar scrawl of my name across the front. I glanced at Trey, and his hand settled on the small of my back, offering support. I moved so that I leaned my back against his chest, pulled the letter out, and let him read over my shoulder.

Hails,

I'm protecting you the only way I can, and that's by leaving. There was a reason why I never told you who I was seeing. Allen is—was—my lover. I know that's hard to hear. It's not easy for me to say, but we can't help who we fall for. And in my case, that meant turning a blind eye to all the sides of him that were so toxic, at least until I couldn't anymore.

His plan was for Trey La Rosa to kill you. And if he didn't, Allen wanted it done another way. He was going to hire someone, and I had to stop him.

You know how much you mean to me. I would give my life for yours if it came down to it. Thank God it didn't. I'm a selfish bastard. We both know that. (You better be laughing.)

But in all seriousness, I couldn't stop Allen no matter how hard I tried. And I did. Trust me on that. Instead, I worked with him because I knew this was your chance with Trey. You know—the guy. The elusive one you dreamed about for over a year but never made a move to meet face-to-face. It was ridiculous to do what we did and even more batshit crazy to pretend to go along with Allen against you.

It worked, though, on my end—you met him. And I know he will find it futile to turn away from you because it's impossible not to fall in love with you.

The seeds of doubt I put in your head when you called after learning of Allen's death were simply me panicking. Trey had nothing to do with it. I never meant to cast blame elsewhere. It was a knee-jerk reaction and the wrong one. I've been doing that a lot lately, something that must change.

There's no way to make up to you for my part in all the wrongs done. So I did the only thing I could: give you the proof I think you needed in that video and make sure Allen never hurt you again.

I'm not coming back. I need a fresh start and to get my head on straight so I don't make the same mistake and fall for the wrong guy again. Besides, I can't wear orange. It's not my color, and we both know it.

It's better this way. Please understand...

I've loved you since the day you punched out my nemesis in the schoolyard and made him bleed. I hope someday you'll be able to forgive me and know that I truly had your best interests at heart, even if it was delivered in a messed-up way.

Always yours,

Justin

I covered my mouth to stop the sobs from filling the room. *He killed Allen.* Trey turned me in his arms and held me tightly. I was aware of the girls, but they let me process. *God, Justin. What did you do? And why didn't you come to me first?*

"Hailey." Sofia's hand rested on my back.

The worst of my tear fest was over. I untangled myself from Trey's arms and accepted the Kleenex she held out to me.

"Is there anything we can do?"

I tried to smile but gave up. That wasn't happening. "No. But thank you."

"We can find him," Trey murmured near my ear.

I tilted my head back, and he straightened. Our gazes locked and held. God, I loved him so much. Concern and determination pulled his chiseled features tight, his strong jawline looking like it could cut glass. "I want that. Not right now, but soon."

"What can I do to help you?"

Take me home. I didn't say it because he could see it written all over my face.

He tore his gaze from mine, scanned the room, and must have made an assessment. "Let's box up what you need and get out of here."

The girls were a tornado of activity. I tucked the letter from Justin with my pictures to deal with later and joined in on getting everything I had to have into a suitcase or box. We were done in under an hour with everything packed into the SUV Trey had driven over. After saying goodbye to my mom, I hugged the girls, making plans for Sunday-night dinner at Emiliana's with everyone. It was a weekly tradition and something I looked forward to but not as much as I did to going back to our place and curling up in Trey's embrace.

We drove home, my hand curled into his, resting on his rock-hard thigh. I took in his strong, confident profile. He was gorgeous, but that wasn't what I loved the most. It was the fact that he had armor on the outside but was all heart on the inside.

He pulled into the condo's underground lot and squeezed my hand. A sense of peace enveloped me. All the tragedy and upset in my life had been a path I was meant to take because it led me to Trey—the other half of my soul.

CHAPTER TWENTY-FIVE

TREY

Modella, Italy
Two weeks later...

Steam swirled around Hailey as she lifted her arm from the hot tub's bubbling water to accept the glass of red wine I held out to her. She took it, and I climbed in. We sat next to one another, facing the sea. I wrapped my arm around her shoulders and pulled her close. The silky slide of her skin against mine almost derailed me from telling her the news I'd learned a few minutes ago.

After Hailey had settled into our place in Chicago, we'd decided a vacation was in order. The family home at Grand Cayman Island was out—Nico was there. My sister had suggested we go to Italy and stay at her and Enzo's place. By the way she pushed the idea, I could tell she was hoping we'd fall in love with it as she had and would buy property as well.

I toyed with a strand of hair that'd escaped Hailey's messy bun, which she'd fashioned on the top of her head. It was chilly at that time of year in Italy but mild compared to the subarctic temperatures back home.

"How does it feel to have more flexibility at the hospital?" Hailey tangled her leg with mine and pulled me from my thoughts.

"Good, it was the right decision." I brushed a few more loose strands behind her ear, captivated by her stunning eyes framed in spikey lashes and the sensual curve of her lips far more than the view spread out before us. "You and my family are what's important to me." Our days weren't guaranteed but a gift. "The flexible schedule suits me better. It gives me the best of both worlds."

"Sofia wants us to find a house here, close to her and Enzo's."

She grinned. "Really? Are you going to?"

"We. As for buying a house here, it's probably a good idea. But I thought you might prefer another location."

"The Caymans?" Her palm rested over my heart, and pink colored her cheeks. "I like it here in Modella but not as much as there. That place means more because of our time there." She shrugged. "I'll probably fall in love with it here when it's warmer and we can hit the beach."

I laughed. Her excitement was palpable, and my decision was made solely on her reaction. She'd loved it there, and I was very fond of the island as well. "Let's look at a few properties while we're here, and then we can fly to the Caymans and get one picked out there too. Or build. That might be a better option."

"Do we have time? I thought Marco said we needed to be back in a few days."

Things were heating up with the New York Mafia syndicate. I needed to be nearby in case anything happened. Marco and I had talked that morning while Hailey lounged in the hot tub. "We have a week. Plenty of time to get started on finding property here and making a call to a realtor in the Caymans."

A shiver ran through Hailey, and she shifted so that she was straddling me, her wine left on the edge of the whirlpool. My hands settled on her waist, and I guided her closer. My resolve was weakening. Soon, I wouldn't be able to resist her. It was always like that with Hailey—one touch, one look, and I was sunk. She'd become my world.

But I had something to say that she deserved to know. "I learned the details of Allen's will this morning."

Her smile, so filled with joy and anticipation, died a swift death. "Why are you telling me this? Allen doesn't have anything to do with me anymore."

That wasn't quite the case. He still tainted her life from beyond the grave. "A life insurance policy was taken out on him a few weeks ago."

"Okay." Wariness flitted across her features.

"His beneficiary was Justine Banks."

Her shoulders physically went down an inch as her body relaxed. "I'm sure Mom isn't happy, but I hardly see how that matters to me."

I ran my hands along her back, enjoying how her skin felt beneath my fingers. Water churned all around us from the jets, and a few drops splashed onto her chest. My gaze trailed their descent, and I longed to follow them with my tongue. I forced myself to focus. "You know why it matters to you."

She sighed, and her eyes drifted shut as she rested her forehead against mine. "Justin or Justine. I get what you're insinuating."

"I know where Justin is."

A tremor ran through her body, and I hugged her to me as she visibly fought the anger at the way her friend was handling things.

"We could go to him." I had to offer, even if I didn't think it was a good idea.

"No." She tangled her hand in my hair. "He needs to get his

life figured out." Her lips brushed over mine, sending jolts of desire through me in their wake. "This is our time."

My hands settled lightly on Hailey's hips. I took in her tempting body and got hung up on her full lips before our gazes met and held. Desire swirled in her green depths, and I glimpsed heaven, exactly where I wanted to spend the remainder of my days. It was the moment I'd waited for, which I thought I'd never have. "The first time we met, I knew you were special. We connected on a deeper level than I'd ever felt before."

Her hands rested flat on my chest, and I knew she felt how fast my heart beat against her palm.

"But the timing wasn't right. It was too soon."

She winked. "It seems fate intervened."

I couldn't help but laugh. Because it had—orchestrated by her and impossible for me to ignore. "I wouldn't have it any other way." I was prepared to spend a lifetime showing her how much she meant to me. "I knew you were the woman for me when you entered that ballroom months ago. I let you slip through my grasp. I won't make that mistake again."

She held still, a quick intake of breath the only sound above the churning water. Wisps of steam rose around us, highlighting her ethereal beauty. "That goes both ways."

Her fierce possessiveness warmed my heart. "I love you, Hailey. Every day with you is a gift. Marry me."

Her lower lip trembled, and raw emotion blazed in her eyes. "I love you, Trey. I think I have since you first spoke to me at the fundraiser. Of course I'll marry you."

I slid my hand up until I cupped the back of her head then slanted my mouth over hers, taking control of the kiss. She melted against me, and I stood in the whirlpool, needing to take her inside so that I could have access to every inch of her body. We had a little less than a week. I planned to give her the world —she certainly had become mine.

The End

Continue reading the Mafia Elite series with RIVALS.
https://amymckinleyauthor.com/mafia-elite/

If you enjoyed reading COLLATERAL DAMAGE as much as I did writing it, I hope you'll consider leaving a review.

RIVALS

RELEASING IN 2022

Nico

I tracked the progression of the approaching storm and the bolts of lightning that pierced the dark clouds. Jagged bolts stabbed the horizon. Electricity charged the air, lending a sense of impending danger. Sea spray misted over me, and the taste of rain permeated every breath. I wanted to stay on the shoreline longer, tempting the fates. But the sting of sand that rode on the increasing strength of the wind caused me to head back, even if only to watch the storm from the lanai.

I turned into the wind and stopped short at the barrel of a 9mm about two feet from my chest. Long black hair tangled in the wind, partially obscuring her face. Recognition rocked me to the soles of my feet. If I had any doubt who it was, that was gone with the flash of violet eyes. Mia Tucci hadn't wanted to be found—until now.

Continue reading the Mafia Elite series with RIVALS.
https://amymckinleyauthor.com/mafia-elite/

ACKNOWLEDGMENTS

The La Rosa family. They've been so much fun to spend time with, and I hope you enjoyed them as much as I have. And we have one more brother—Nico. I'm so excited for you to read his story too. But I'm jumping ahead, and there are so many people that I'm so lucky to have there for me through the Mafia world journey. I couldn't do it without them.

First and foremost, my family. Their support and encouragement are humbling. I am beyond grateful.

Thank you to the most amazing critique partners, friends, and fellow authors: Candace Irvin and Kristin Kisska. Their willingness to dive into the trenches with me and read these stories, offering creative input, is invaluable.

I have a fabulous editorial team from Red Adept Editing: Kate Birdsall and Taylor Anhalt. They do a fantastic job of shaping the story into what it is today. I couldn't do this without them!

And these covers—T.E. Black Designs—thank you for understanding my vision and turning it into a design that exceeds my expectations.

Two people that have been in my corner for some time now —Colleen Noyes with Itsy Bitsy Book Bits, and Danielle Sanchez with Wildfire Marketing Solutions—who work hard to make each release a success. Thank you for all that you do!

Last but certainly not least, a special thank you to all the incredible bloggers and readers who have encouraged and

helped me along the way and who continue to make my dream
a reality.

Thank you.

ABOUT THE AUTHOR

Amy McKinley is the *USA Today* bestselling author of the romantic suspense thriller Gray Ghost Novels, Deadly Isles Special Ops, Covert Recruits, Mafia Elite, Verretti Crime Family, Moonlit Destination Series, the Five Fates paranormal romance books, and several standalone titles. Her edge-of-your-seat books are filled with surprising twists and just the right amount of heat and danger. She lives in Illinois with her husband, two daughters, two sons, and three mischievous cats.

You can find her at:
www.AmyMcKinley.com

Subscribe to Amy's newsletter for cover reveals, book announcements, and giveaways: https://bit.ly/3CGcdSF

goodreads.com/amymckinley_author
bookbub.com/authors/amy-mckinley
facebook.com/amymckinleyauthor
instagram.com/amymckinleyauthor

ALSO BY AMY MCKINLEY

<u>Gray Ghost Novels</u>

Moments That Define Us

Broken Circle

Eye of the Storm

Beneath the Surface

Vantage Point

Covert Threat

Marked for Death

-

<u>Deadly Isles Special Ops</u>

Twisted Secrets

Bound by Secrets

Forged by Secrets

-

Mafia Elite

No Way Out

Blood Oath

Born in Darkness

Savage Secrets

Ruthless Heir

Collateral Damage

Rivals

-

Verretti Crime Family (coming soon)

Borrowed Time

My Enemy's Bed

Fractured Lies

-

Covert Recruits (coming soon)

Irina

Sasha

Zena

Nadia

Katya

-

Standalone Titles

Shattered Melody

Siren's Call: Cursed Seas

Fake Fiancé (A Second Chance Office Romance)

-

Moonlit Destination Series

Moonlit Whisper

Moonlit Kiss

Moonlit Mirage

Five Fates Series

Hidden

Taken